Burton Harrison

A bachelor maid

With illustrations by Irving R. Wiles

Burton Harrison

A bachelor maid
With illustrations by Irving R. Wiles

ISBN/EAN: 9783743308862

Manufactured in Europe, USA, Canada, Australia, Japa

Cover: Foto ©Andreas Hilbeck / pixelio.de

Manufactured and distributed by brebook publishing software
(www.brebook.com)

Burton Harrison

A bachelor maid

"'IT NEEDED ONLY THIS!' SHE CRIED." (SEE PAGE 118.)

A BACHELOR MAID

BY MRS. BURTON HARRISON

AUTHOR OF "CROW'S NEST AND BELHAVEN TALES," "SWEET BELLS
OUT OF TUNE," ETC.

WITH ILLUSTRATIONS BY

IRVING R. WILES

NEW YORK: THE CENTURY CO.
1899

LIST OF ILLUSTRATIONS.

	PAGE
"'IT NEEDED ONLY THIS!' SHE CRIED"	*Frontispiece*
MR. JUSTICE IRVING	5
GORDON	13
MARION	27
"THEY WERE A PLEASING CONTRAST"	59
"PERHAPS WE OUGHT NOT TO DISTURB YOU"	151
"MARION CAME AT ONCE"	183

I

R. JUSTICE IRVING was in the act of putting on his overcoat to leave the Antediluvian Club. He was feeling reasonably cheerful, for he had beaten his favorite adversary, Bob Crouch, at billiards; so cheerful, indeed, that he made a mental note of a fleeting resolve to give Crouch, to console him, the next appointment he should have of a commissioner in lunacy.

It was, therefore, a smiling countenance his honor turned upon a young man already equipped for the street, who came to offer him a hand with his coat.

"Ha, Gordon! That you? Have n't seen you before this evening."

"No; I have just come in, hoping to catch you — and to walk home with you, if I may."

"Glad of your company, my dear boy," the judge said, as they emerged under the sparkling heaven of a mild winter's night in New York. "Wanted to speak to you about the sale of Romaine's books. What the deuce he means by selling them, I can't make out. Twenty good years of a man's life put into a collection that can't be beat for choiceness, and here they are to be scattered for a freak. You must manage to be there, my dear lad; there are one or two tidbits my mouth has been watering for this age. You must appear for me, as usual, and mind you secure them, if I am to die in peace. And I've got a copy of the new Prayer-Book, édition de luxe, to show you, with a story attached to it as good, almost, as my luck in getting it half price. Did n't see you at the Grolier last night, by the way. Were you and Marion quarreling, as usual, at our house? Can't think where that daughter of mine gets her way of flying off the handle about little things not quite to her taste."

"She has flown off the handle for good and all, so far as I am concerned," said the young lawyer. "She has broken our engagement."

"Broken — your — oh — good heaven, Gordon, you are thirty years old — you are not taken in by stuff like that? Broken — the girl 's mad; I always said so; that woman's college I was fool enough to send her to — to 'finish her education,' forsooth! — has put more silly rot into her head than it ever did ideas. Ever since she quitted it, four years ago, she has gone on following one fad after the other, till I 'm thankful she has n't brought me to be an open laughing-stock before the town. And what this means, I don't believe anybody knows. She took you of her own free will; you 've been engaged a year; and I had every hope of seeing her married, and settled, and out of mischief, in the spring — and —" here his honor emitted a naughty word, and struck his stick upon the pavement so fiercely that a policeman, accidentally in his place upon the block, looked around with languid interest to see what was "up"—"she *shall* marry you in the spring, or I 'll know the reason why."

"Marion would not be the prize I have thought her," said the young man, modestly, "if she could be forced into marrying against her will."

"What 's her will? What does a girl know about what she wants, and what she does n't want?" pursued the irate father. "If there 's anything on God's earth troublesome to deal with at the breakfast-table, or on the witness-stand, it 's a woman. Troublesome? Exasperating? *Devilish!* If ever I lost my temper, it would be with the whimwhams miscalled woman's ideas. This age is going to pot with 'em. The creatures write (and, what 's worse, print!), and howl and shriek on platforms, and struggle for equality with us in a perfectly disgusting way. It 's some one of that gang that 's got hold of Marion, you may depend; that 's persuaded her she has a mission above matrimony. If that were the case, and I had my way, I 'd like to sentence the offender to be ducked as a common scold."

Gordon had foreseen the effect of his communication. He waited quietly, adjusting his long strides to the somewhat shorter and heavier ones of his senior, until the first access of anger had talked itself out, and then took up the tale in the same even, self-controlled voice in which he had begun it.

"I don't suppose it 's worth while for me to tell you how long I 've wanted Marion. She is five-and-twenty now; I took my love for her into the law-school with me, and have never wavered in it since.

I did not ask her till a year ago, because I had n't enough to offer her till then."

"Egad, man, you 've made a hit at our bar second to none of your contemporaries; and I 'm blessed if I know one of them that 's got an eye and a *flair* like yours for a good book. You are the only man alive I 'd wish to have come in for my library when I 'm gone. I have left it to you in my will, as you know, with the stipulation it 's to be kept together."

"That can now no longer be my duty, sir," answered Gordon.

"Alec, what are you thinking of? Why, if twenty Marions threw you overboard, you 'd still have *the books!*" exclaimed his honor, with heartfelt emphasis. "But, come, tell me about this business quietly; don't excite yourself. In such matters nothing is gained by losing our grip on our tempers. When did she give you this precious piece of information? Broken her engagement, eh? I 'll be hanged if I 'll put up with such scurvy treatment of her father's wishes. Am I nobody in my own house, I 'd like to know? Am I a cipher, a petticoat-ridden judge, at the mercy of a spoiled girl infected with all the worst notions about woman's independence in our day — a — ?"

"I received, yesterday, a note from her," Gordon said, taking advantage of a pause during which the judge was fortunately obliged to blow his nose, "telling me that she was thoroughly unhappy in the existing relations — which, indeed, I had perceived. She asked me to go to her last evening, and I went. We talked over the subject in every aspect possible. I said everything a man in my circumstances could

MR. JUSTICE IRVING.

say. She looked more beautiful than I have ever seen her, and she was neither over-excited, nor exaggerated in her speech —"

"Marion *is* like me, they tell me," interpolated the father, grimly smiling in the dark.

"But there was no deceiving myself. Marion's ideas have undergone a change. She has come to this conclusion deliberately. She did not need to remind me that she, unlike most girls, had begun her life in society without holding marriage as its chief goal —"

"Stuff and nonsense! If you can find anything in the world as dismal and depressing as a woman, outside of a sisterhood, who devotes herself, through conviction, to a single life — they 're bad enough, and vexatious enough, married; but as old maids — and if I 've got to pass the remainder of my days in the cage with one of them! I won't do it, Gordon; I won't do it! I 'll box up the books, send them to a safety deposit company, let my house, take rooms near the club, and allow Miss Irving to enjoy her single blessedness where she will."

"Don't decide now, sir," said Gordon, who, not in the least surprised at the father's attitude, pursued the even tenor of his way. "What I want to ask you — as a favor to me, if you consider that I am at all injured or aggrieved by the turn affairs have taken — is to say nothing to Marion. I told her that I would tell you of her dismissal of me."

"It 's the first time I ever knew her to be a coward!"

"She is no coward; and you do not think so," Gordon said, a little rise in his temperature making itself manifest in his voice. "She is as brave a girl as ever drew breath, and as true. I asked her leave to tell you — I want you to prove your friendship for me, sir — that I 've never had cause to doubt — that is my honor and my pride —"

"You 'd have been the son I 'd have chosen, Alec, to make up for the boy I lost," said the older man, and the two gripped hands on it.

"You won't scold her — you won't visit it on her in any way? You will accept it, as I do, as final? You will gratify any wish of hers to shape her life according to the ambition she now has?"

"You ask a good lot of me, Alec. I did not see her this morning. Come to think of it, they said she had a headache, and Marion never has headaches; and I dined at the club with Crouch and a couple of Western lawyers he has on hand. Crouch plays a pretty good game at billiards, Alec, eh? Not many men in the Antediluvian who can lay him out. Well, I beat him three times running to-night. Poor return for his capital dinner, eh? By George, that chef can cook ducks! Outside, a beautiful, even brown, and the blood following the knife — cooked to a charm. And with them we had a glass of Chambertin just the right temperature. Say what you will, those things tell. Give me rather a chop and a bottle of beer if I can't get ducks roasted right, which you never can in your own house, I 've found. I 'm the easiest fellow to please in all the world, but when that woman of Marion's sends up wild ducks overdone! You were saying you want me not to haul Marion over the coals. Why, Alec, you know if there 's anything I don't do, it is to let myself loose when anything vexes me."

"I know," ventured Gordon, soothingly. "But as this is rather more vexing than usual, I want to be sure Marion does not suffer because I have been telling tales on her. Let her speak to you first, if speak of it you must between you. Allow everything to go on as before. If you could think of some one to invite to make her a visit at this time, it would take her out of herself, and break up her solitude, which can't be good for her just now."

"Solitude? What does she expect? She's mistress of a good house, with plenty of servants, leave to go and come, a carriage and a maid to take her into society. She has more invitations than she cares to accept. I can't fill up the house with chattering women, to please her. Good Lord! They'd be turning over my neckties, and even handling the books, before you'd know it! But I'll agree to say nothing. That I can do. It's no sacrifice to me not to speak my mind out."

"Thank you," said Gordon, briefly. They were now stopping in front of the judge's house, a broad, comfortable mansion of red brick a few doors from Fifth Avenue, in an old-fashioned, pleasant quarter not far from the Marble Arch. While the judge was feeling for his latch-key, Gordon managed to look up unobserved at the windows of the third story above him. From the angle made by the curtains in one of these upon a shade illuminated from within, he saw a shadow withdraw. He knew this room to be the special belonging of his lately affianced wife, and he

recoguized the stately outline of her figure. She,
then, had been waiting and watching for her father,
when all the rest of the quiet house was in darkness.
Gordon remembered, with a pang of sympathy for
her, that in all the world outside that sleeping house
she had no friend but himself who knew her as she
was, who was familiar with the daily trials of her lot,
who could stand between her and them. And now
she had voluntarily put him from her, to live alone
and to fight her own battles with what he believed
to be a world of shadows summoned by her over-
vivid imagination to people the loneliness of her
life.

Not anger, but a vast pity for Marion, took fresh
possession of him.

"Good night, then, Alec, if you won't come in and
look at that catalogue of Romaine's books," said the
judge in his loud, clear, self-satisfied voice.

"Not to-night. I think if you or Marion could
think of any place where she might like to go for a
little change — any one going abroad whom she
might join —"

"Go abroad! Not by a jugful," said his honor,
vexed into a slang phrase. "I've no patience with
these female vagrants who leave the houses provided
for them, and the duties of their proper sphere, to go
wandering around in foreign parts amusing themselves like tramps. Marion knows that, when I am
able to get off, she goes with *me* under *my* charge, to
do the things *I* think best for her; and with that she
has got to be content. Oh, these women, Alec —
these women nowadays! They never are content;

they are as mischievous an element in our society as anarchists. Look at my mother — wife of a country parson, brought up six sons in a Massachusetts village, toiled and struggled for them, never thought of herself, I believe, till she lay down to rest in the old graveyard. Look at Marion's mother — ill health from the time Marion was born, and she never let me know it, except in a general way, until she died. Those *were* women; Marion's degenerate —"

"I won't keep you in the draft of the open door," Gordon went on, with the quiet persistence that was a part of him. "But I hope, if Marion has any friend she desires to visit her, you will think well of providing her with a companion. Just now she needs distraction for her thoughts. She will be safer with some outlet."

"Well, well, I'll think of it. Good night. Come over on Sunday afternoon as usual, and stop to dinner, and we'll go over Romaine's catalogue carefully. You are not going to let this girl's folly rob me of you, my boy?"

"Good night, sir," the young man said. He had grown into the habit of thus addressing him as a father.

Again they shook hands, the front door closed, and Gordon ran down the steps to the sidewalk. Instead of going home, however, he crossed the street, walking up and down, and looking from time to time over at the window of Marion's sitting-room. When the lights there were extinguished, he turned into the Avenue, and made his way to his quarters in Washington Square.

In the corridor leading to his rooms he met a man of his acquaintance, likewise on his way into retreat.

"Hullo, Gordon! Saw you leaving the Antediluvian a while ago arm-in-arm with your father-in-law elect. I stopped behind to enter my third remonstrance on one subject in the complaint-book. There's a plot among the club-servants to smile whenever I make observations about the ventilation of the rooms; and, by George, if the governors don't take some notice of it, I'll resign out of the club. Been seeing his honor home, eh? Soft thing you have there, old fellow; not to speak of the references that drop into your path like 'the gentle dew from heaven.' When are you going to hang up your hat for good upon Irving J.'s hat-rack?"

"Miss Irving's engagement to me is at an end, Clarkson," said Gordon, pausing at his own door, and speaking deliberately, while holding his handsome head erect, and looking his interlocutor full in the face.

"What?" said Clarkson, genuinely surprised.

"Yes," answered Gordon.

"Is there—if any one asks me the reason, what would you like me to say, old man?"

"Say that it has been dissolved by mutual consent. Good night to you." And, opening his door, Gordon disappeared abruptly from the view of his acquaintance, who was left upon the mat, whistling softly.

"FATHER, I have been sitting up for you," Marion had said, following the judge into his library, whither he went directly upon entering his home.

GORDON.

This room, containing the apple of Judge Irving's eye, was at the back of the house, in an extension built to receive it over the dining-room. Upon its walls, everywhere — save for the projecting jamb of a great chimneypiece of carved oak, and a bay-window, the upper half of thin glass veined with delicate traceries of lead, the lower curtained with amber silk, making sunshine in the gloom — were seen the mellow bindings of "the books." The books, Marion's rivals, were best loved, as she knew, for their outer integument, for their rare press-marks, for the fact that another collector had failed to secure them. Into these had gone a liberal part of the income insured to Mr. Irving during his life by his wife's will, setting aside for her daughter, after she should have reached the age of twenty-five, an annual allowance of three thousand dollars.

Marion, having just passed the period indicated, had not as yet touched her inheritance. Her father had reluctantly acceded to his wife's desire so to dispose of her own belongings. Although he would have furiously repudiated the idea of having influenced his spouse in the matter of a will so largely in his favor, poor meek Mrs. Irving, going to her grave at a gallop, took care to obtain from her husband information as to the exact age at which he was willing their daughter should begin to enjoy an independence of the purse; and, somehow or other, twenty-five was the age given to the lawyer who drew up the document.

"I am glad you fixed upon five and twenty, Angela," the judge had said approvingly, after the poor

lady's last will and testament had been duly signed
and witnessed. "It is an evidence of your excellent
judgment, my dear. You know very well that no
young woman, before that age, should be regarded as
a responsible being, or have tools for folly or mis-
chief-making put into her hands. Yes; I am glad
you thought of it — very glad."

Whereon he had stooped over her couch, and
kissed her, going out of her room in such fullness of
vigor and manly good-looks that she felt, in the heart
already gripped by death, a gentle palpitation of her
old adoring love for him. A little later she went to
her reward, satisfied that she had done her best by
the daughter left in the care of such an infallible
being.

These things had passed when Marion was a child
of twelve. At eighteen she had been a woman, ardent, thoughtful, speculative, but ever since had lived
the life of an infant in leading-strings, so far as her
father was concerned. The curriculum he had allowed her to take at a woman's college in a neighbor-
ing State had been her one opportunity to stand
alone, to test the little budding wings of her intellect,
to speak upon any subject of the outer world without
the certainty that she would be crushed, or smiled
down upon, according to his mood.

Thus the engagement with Alec Gordon, entered
into by her with hesitation in response to his fervent
pleadings, was poisoned at its source. She had
learned to look upon man as an oppressor of woman;
to mistrust him as morally weak when physically
most attractive; to resent the domestic law-giver; to

dread giving up liberty, even comparative, for the positive slavery of marriage. Her father's favorite saying, in response to any remark of hers he found it inconvenient to answer,—"When Gordon gets hold of you, he will take all that nonsense out of you, my dear,"—had grown to be the nightmare of her engagement. And at last, little by little, the solitary self-tormenting of the girl had worn away her power to discriminate in character. She could see in her lover only her father's instrument. In her despair, she wrote to a friend who had been a professor in the college, and told her the case as if it had been that of some one else. Of the answer we will quote this phrase:

In sum, I should say to your friend that if her God-sent intentions were followed out by all women who experience them, we should be moving with quick strides to the future we pray for, when man through woman shall be made to know himself.

"I am not sure I know what she advises," quoth poor Marion, who had been reading seven pages preceding the sentence quoted. "But she feels for me. If I could talk with her in person, I should be easier. Oh, what in my place would the Higher Woman do?"

What Marion did we have learned from Alec Gordon's lips. It now remained for her to meet the storm of her father's wrath. She came into the library, swiftly, tragically, her tall form carrying the sweep of a loose white robe edged with brown fur. A band of the same fur, clasping her throat, repeated the tint of her massive hair, parted in an exquisite clean line, and twisted in a coil behind. This, as did

everything about the physical woman of Marion
Irving, illustrated nature unspoiled by conventionality. Her taper waist, her small bust, her grand
arms, her free movements, were the delight of a
sketch-class of girls to which she belonged. When
she would consent to sit for them, there was a general
exclamation — a long-drawn "Oh!" of satisfaction,
deep, not loud. Once, draped in cheese-cloth dam-
pened and dried into the beautiful pliability beloved
by an artist, she had posed for them in the attitude
of the "Winged Victory of Samothrace." Her superb
appearance on the platform in this guise was followed
by an enthusiastic burst of applause from the class
that covered the model with a veil of blushes.

Of the bewitchments of ordinary feminine beauty
she possessed few. She had no coquetry, no desire to
test her power on men. Her father's unfeigned con-
tempt of all varieties of female supremacy had made
her mistrust her ability either to charm or to command. She was singularly simple, direct, outspoken,
and by men of society, so called, was rather eschewed
than otherwise.

As she now descended upon her father, she found
him warming himself, with his back to a cozy little
fire, its flame many times repeated in a setting of yellow tiles. On the table beside his deep arm-chair
cushioned with old-blue corduroy (these blues and
yellows carefully chosen by himself) stood a reading-
lamp, and a tray with a small cut-glass decanter of
spirits and a plate of biscuits. The butler had seen,
according to custom, that everything was in place.
The judge meant to sit there for a quiet half-hour

before retiring, to enjoy the consciousness of good health, good looks, good digestion, good repute, and a good balance at the bank.

Marion's appearance surprised him unpleasantly. A domestic whirlwind, in the wee sma' hours, when a man has nowhere to flee from it, is indeed a fearsome sight. Why in the dickens, he asked himself, could not the girl have put off this business till morning, when it is always possible to cut short the heat of any discussion by opening the front door? He frowned, therefore. His eyes surveyed her with the cold displeasure she so easily aroused. He was the Mr. Justice Irving Marion knew best, not the clever, genial Mr. Justice Irving known to the bar and public.

"You know I cannot endure having any one sit up for me. You have repeatedly heard me say so to the butler and the maids."

"I know, father, I know. I will never do so again. But I felt I could not go to sleep another night, not having told you that I have broken with Alec Gordon."

"You may spare yourself the words, and me the annoyance. Gordon walked home with me and told me. If I had to hear it, it was better coming from a man who can tell a straight story than from a woman who dresses the whole thing up to suit herself—"

"Stop!" she cried. "Not that! In all my life I never told you a lie."

"There you go, taking offense at trifles, as usual. I meant, of course, that you would naturally want to put the best face on this shameful business."

"There is no shame in refusing to marry a man I am afraid I may grow to hate. The shame would be standing at the altar by him, and swearing false oaths. I want to put no face on it except the true one. I have searched my heart, father, for the love a wife ought to bear her husband, if married life is to be supportable—"

"Come, come!" said the judge, rather scandalized.

"I have found there nothing but a cold, hard crust of indifference. I like Alec as a friend; I tried to love him: but I love no one. Father—" she paused, a mighty swelling of the heart took away her speech for a moment; she drew near and, rare act, laid her hand upon his shoulder—"father, you *do* understand me, don't you? You loved once—did n't you?"

The judge, uncertain whether to be angrier than he already was, or to treat the matter as a very insignificant joke, moved away from her hand.

"I—why, Marion, I am astonished at you—I—bless my soul, what won't women try to investigate in these days—I believe your mother had no cause of complaint against me as a husband. But then *she* was one of the kind who take things as they find them, who don't tear the passions to tatters, and go back to the fundamental basis of created things when a hasty word is spoken. She was an admirable woman, and her loss—er—ah—" here the judge, catching sight of a newly arrived express-parcel upon the table, expanded into a positive smile of rapture. "By the Great Horn Spoon! if there's not the 'Gesta Romanorum' from that Boston sale!"

"May I finish, father?" said Marion, her arms fall

ing dead, as her father seized, gloatingly, upon his prize.

"If it's *quite* the same to you, my dear Marion, we'll remit the rest until breakfast-time to-morrow. I had made an offer for this, but feared Lewis, who was on the spot, would outbid me. Oh, by the way, on Saturday I shall have leisure — you shall have your bank-book and check-book, and I'll explain to you how to use them. And, Marion," he added, turning over affectionately the saffron-hued leaves of the little volume, "that reminds me, if you would like to have a visit from any friend — how would it do to invite my brother Joe's girls over from Philadelphia for a week?"

"They have gone to Montreal, father," she said listlessly. Even the threat of a visit from her Uncle Joe's girls — pretty, flippant creatures, forever agog after men and finery — could not shock her now.

"Then think for yourself — there must be somebody," he suggested, already a little out of patience, and longing to be alone.

"I have a friend — a widow; she was for a time a teacher in our college, and left it to be married. She is now in Washington, unoccupied and very poor, I believe."

"And, pray, what is her name?" he said, turning over the leaves as before.

"Stauffer — Madame Stauffer, they call her, since her husband was a foreigner. She is not old, and rather nice-looking. She would interest me, I think."

"Then for Heaven's sake ask her, and be done with it. Only, when she gets here, mind, I break-

2

fast alone, and dine at the club whenever the fancy takes me."

"I understand."

She waited a minute, but he did not again notice her. Marion left the room, in spite of herself a trifle lighter of heart than when she came into it. She remembered Sara Stauffer's gift of sympathy. She was at last to have some one, all her own, unshared by her father, uninfluenced by his views and wishes.

Before going to bed, she glanced again at the letter received from Sara a few days before. She decided that she would not wait to write, but early next morning would send a telegram inviting Madame Stauffer to be her guest.

Marion, warmed with new hope, was still thinking of Sara Stauffer when, by extinguishing the gas, she did what, unknown to her, was the signal for Alec Gordon to turn away from his watchman's beat on the pavement over the way, and to go back to his quarters, carrying the keenest disappointment of his life.

II

FEW days after the permission given to his daughter in the first glow of satisfaction at acquiring an almost unique copy of the "Gesta Romanorum," Judge Irving, coming home to dinner, stumbled, upon his own threshold, over an expressman carrying in a little trunk.

"Here, you! There's some mistake. That is not for this number," he called out to the man, who was blocking the way ahead of him.

"I beg your pardon, sir," interposed the footman, who held open the heavy old mahogany door with its side-lights, fan-light, and brass knocker, bespeaking the antique respectability intrenched behind it. "It's the luggage of the furren lady that's come to visit Miss Irving. Hurry up, my man!" he added in a lower tone. "Look sharp for the gas-fixture, and carry that little article to the third-story back. Maid's on the stairs to show you."

"Third-story back?" repeated the master of the house, who was all ears for everything that went on inside of it. "That is Miss Irving's own bedroom, Hilary."

"Them was Miss Irving's orders, sir. Miss Irving have moved into the small room for the present."

"Very extraordinary," muttered the judge, rather pleased with a grievance to cover the extreme annoyance he had felt at sight of the little trunk.

An impertinent little trunk — small, cramped-looking, not by any means of the appearance to justify its ascent of *his* front stairs — the kind of trunk habitually delivered after nightfall by cheap expressmen at the basement door, as appertaining to one of the ladies of divers nationalities who arrive at one's home, and remain for a time, "until suited," with their clothes in a paper parcel.

Mr. Justice Irving, whose appearance on the bench presented a majesty felt alike by lawyers, clients, and court-officers, had a dim idea that he had detected on the countenance of his servant, when the offending box had come under his august observation, an expression of pleased appreciation.

"So Miss Irving has changed her bedroom? And this lady — when did she arrive?"

"About four-thirty, sir. Walked over from the elevated, sir, I understood. I took tea in, almost immediately, to Miss Irving's sitting-room, where the ladies has been talkin' ever since."

"I remember, now," said his master, frowning upon his affability. "It *was* to-day she — that pers — the lady, was to arrive. Hilary, I shall dine at the club. You can mention it to Miss Irving, just before dinner is served, so that she may not wait for me."

"Very good, sir," said Hilary, hanging up the judge's coat and smiling more freely as the broad back of his master ascended the stairs to his dressing-room.

But, after all, what was there to smile at? Any man in Judge Irving's circumstances would have had just cause for a desire to flee. His privacy invaded, the silence of his home broken, by a little Madame Nobody, who had been trumped up by his daughter when in one of her hysterical moods. A little person —that she was little he decided from her trunk— who would require civility, before whom he must needs curb his tongue into the platitudes expected by women at meal-times. A "queer" person, he was sure; a genius of the provinces; a bore, in short—a fearful, unmitigated bore!

And add all this to the natural unwillingness of the male sovereign to face in his domestic kingdom a stranger who would expect him to live up to his reputation for dignity and agreeability. He thought, while tying his white cravat, of the occasion when Charlotte Brontë had arrived to dine with Thackeray, and *that* great man was discovered by his daughters in the act of escaping from the house to seek the seclusion of *his* club. No; this was really too much for even Marion's selfishness to impose on him, and he should take care not to delay in making her understand the ordeal was not to last.

MEANWHILE, the afternoon that Marion felt to be an epoch in her existence had flown by, for the women, on happy wings. Sara, arriving by some mischance unexpectedly, had been met, greeted, installed by Marion in her own easiest chair in her own sanc-

tum, petted, looked after, in a way that expanded the
stranger's heart with wonder.

What a transition for Madame Stauffer — from the
hall-bedroom of a dingy boarding-house in Washington to the heart of this broad, luxurious, esthetic
home, where life ran on well-oiled wheels, where flowers and sunshine banished winter, where the delicious
scent of burning hickory arose from the fireplaces,
where books and pamphlets, old and new, were scattered on all sides!

Sara, who by nature dearly loved easy-chairs and
sweet odors and warm sunshine, and by theory as
well as necessity renounced them, was for a moment
staggered, at the outset of her visit to her old pupil.

She had not, for some reason, counted upon all this.
Marion, always simple in her dress and habits, had
been, while in college, under the yoke of a period of
self-denial. Everything not absolutely necessary had
been by her vowed to students poorer than herself,
to philanthropic or charitable enterprises nurtured
among them. And, since Miss Irving's father had
never thought it wise to give her the control of funds,
her scanty pocket-money had not gone far in the direction indicated. Her want of finery had often been
discussed among her fellows. She was, in fact, regarded as one of the students kept in college by an
effort on the part of their parents or guardians.

Madame Stauffer, after weighing against the price
of board in Washington the expense of a railway
journey to New York, had decided that the affair,
even if Marion's way of living were rather pinched,
would be "worth while." A two weeks' stay would

MARION.

justify her outlay. And for many reasons Sara had long and ardently desired a visit to the great metropolis. She was of the army of modern thinkers who declare, " Better a garret in New York " than a first-floor bedroom in the " half-baked " cities elsewhere to be found in America—an expression for which Madame Stauffer's class must stand responsible.

In the short time that had elapsed since her arrival, Sara had been put into possession of the chief facts of her friend's recent experience of the heart; of Marion's doubts, fears, and ambitions for a more fully developed intellectual existence; of her difficulty in finding true sympathy with her aims among the people she was cast with; of her conviction that there was a key to the higher philosophy of living, if she could only lay hand on it; of her longing to be something—if it were but a unit—in the great cause of the evolution of true womanhood.

Madame Stauffer, a slight, pleasing woman of thirty-one or -two, with dark, diamond-bright eyes and an irradiating smile, looked down from her throne among the cushions on the corner of Marion's divan next the fire, at the noble, earnest, dilating creature seated upon a low stool at her feet. They had dressed for dinner, and returned to wait in the drawing-room till that meal should be announced.

In her room — Marion's room vacated for her — Sara, left alone, had sped from object to object of its luxurious furnishings, examining them curiously. She had even turned up a corner of the old Genoese coverlet of flowered cotton edged with antique lace, to see the silk lining underneath.

"Cotton on top, silk underneath! That is the real thing! When could I have afforded such?" she said, with a pang of envy. "Every thread of silk in my life has done duty before the public — exhibited for all it was worth!"

The couch, the writing-table, the sundry mirrors, the bath-room opening out of Marion's bower, had seemed to her unbelievable.

"A porcelain tub, all to myself, with white tiles underfoot, has always seemed to me something intended for the angels," she murmured whimsically. "And towels like these! Long, fine, hemstitched, abundant! Oh, it is too much; I must shut the door, and not think of the bath-room, or my brain can't be depended upon to do its duty and pay for the privilege of using all this!"

She had put on the one best gown of the traditional poor heroine, and, opening the door into the corridor, had found Marion waiting there for her, with a fresh bunch of purple violets. There is no heart, however cold, case-hardened, worldly, that cannot be touched by the humanizing offer of a bunch of fresh violets. They are the open sesame to every woman's affections; on their breath arise the most tender beseechings to loving-kindness; under their influence the recipient longs to do, say, be something delightful to the giver.

Sara Stauffer almost cried when she took these from the hand of Marion. It was the finishing touch to her newly erected dream-temple of comfort and beauty combined. She kissed the tall girl, inclining her face upward to do so, and, twining her arm round her waist, exclaimed, as they went down-stairs:

"O Marion, how perfectly happy we are going to be!"

And now Marion, whom nothing could long divert from her intense purpose, had reverted to asking Sara's advice.

"Do you mean that you want to go in for public utterances?" Sara answered, vaguely thinking how hard it would be to leave this nest of cushions by the fire in behalf of the suffering sisterhood.

"For speaking?" said Marion, a little startled, yet dazzled visibly. "Oh, I should never be allowed, *never!* After you have seen, you will know."

"Writing over your own name? As your father's daughter, that would mean much."

"Even if I dared to think of that, Sara—for you are not madame to me, are you, any longer? You are my friend, my teacher; you are going to be my sister spirit. Think of a woman of twenty-five saying, 'If I dared do what my conscience tells me is right!' But as long as I live here under his roof, supported by my father, I can do so little: I could write anonymously, I suppose."

"There are so many who write well whose names don't count," answered Sara, as if with an effort. She had just caught sight of Marion's beautiful, shapely foot extended upon the hearth-rug; of its casing of fine black silken openwork, its high-heeled slipper of patent leather, with a small buckle of brilliants. And Sara, who had a charming foot of her own, did so love pretty shoes and stockings, and had had so few of them! "Perhaps we can work out between us some method for you to serve the Cause."

"Oh, how gladly would I do so! If I might, how

gladly would I give up all this cramping luxury, to go out and work for and with my sisters, as you have done!"

"It is a hard life. I have lectured so much in the last year, and traveled so far, that my physician ordered me to rest in the comparatively mild climate of Washington," said Madame Sara, with a faint sigh.

"Poor thing!" said Marion, with a heartfelt sigh. "And so you divined at once that, in the hypothetical crisis my first letter laid before you, I was stating my own case?"

"Yes, dear child," answered Sara, caressingly. "And to tell you the candid truth, I was a little afraid to handle it freely, as you asked me to do."

"Well, it is all settled now. You can speak out now. As I told you a little while ago, I am already happier to be free from the torment of wondering if I loved him enough to accept, for his sake, the further limitations marriage would set around me."

"Is he — is he — good-looking, dear child?" Sara asked, burying her little nose in her violets, as if she could not get enough of their fragrance.

"I suppose you would think so," answered the girl. "He is on rather a large scale; but most people call him handsome."

"And successful — sure to rise?"

Marion was a little surprised. In the college days Sara had affected to scorn mere externals in mankind, to hold them as naught beside the gold of heart and mind.

"I believe people say he is," she said almost coldly.

"I was only trying to gage the depth of your renunciation, my love. In these days what they call a good match is so hard to find, and the world is so hard upon women struggling for themselves, it is almost heroism to renounce a safe marriage. But you — what am I thinking of? Your future is secure beyond peradventure. You, no matter what knocks and thumps you may get from the public, will have the sinews of war provided. You have only to be brave and steadfast, and in time all things will come to you."

"*Do* you think so?" cried Marion, exultingly.

"I do. Just now, while you are still young and nominally under your father's control, you can work for the 'Woman Question' alone. By and by you will reach, and be able to handle, the broader phase of it, the 'Marriage Question,' which is, after all, or is sure to absorb, the 'Woman Question.'"

"I don't quite understand," said Marion, her sweet, innocent eyes a little clouded by bewilderment.

"No; but there is time enough for that," said Sara, nestling down with fresh abandonment among the pillows. "Those of us who are victims of the horrible mistake of marriage with men we could not possibly know as they were may be left in charge of that branch of the subject. I see you are too much afraid of wounding me to ask if that was, indeed, my case. Some day I will tell you at length my experience, luckily brief. My husband, a German professor I met at a friend's house in Chicago, and married three weeks later, died of yellow fever in the South at the end of a year, six months of which we had spent apart. From these dates you may see my bondage did not long endure. But it has left in me an ineffaceable sense of wrong, and, having told you so much, I will not darken the enjoyment of the hour by elaborating on the theme."

"Don't tell me, you poor dear!" cried Marion. "I am sure that, whoever was wrong, you were right; that you did everything noble, grand, and true."

At this juncture the door opened. Madame Stauffer, who had paused to adjust an answer to Marion's enthusiastic speech was prevented from uttering it by the appearance of Hilary, conveying the judge's message to his daughter.

"Not going to dine with us!" exclaimed the new arrival, in what Hilary decided to be "a forward way, considerin'."

"Of course you understand, dear girl," the lady went on, as they, directly afterward, walked in to dinner, "that, having come here as special physician in your case, I am all impatience to possess myself of it in every detail. Until I know your father, and see you with him, I cannot pretend to say how far you ought to venture in maintaining our ideas about free womanhood. Until now my time has been almost exclusively occupied with wives, not daughters. My mission is to overcome the isolation of the married woman, to reclaim her into an understanding of her rights, to show her there are other things to absorb her every waking thought than the mere subserviency to a husband — the mere bringing into the world, and up in the world, of children. Your case, being novel, interests me greatly. Yours is a thraldom from which even your liberal education has not been able to free you —"

At this moment Madame Stauffer dipped her spoon into her soup, and a mouthful of velvety *crème de céleri* found its way to her palate.

The Swedish dame who presided over the stewpans of Mr. Justice Irving was, in her way, a gem. In spite of his animadversions upon her habit of misunderstanding the divine canvasback, he knew, and everybody knew, she could be trusted to send up dinners not to be outdone at any of his clubs. For the two ladies she had prepared a few selected *plats* only; but they were cooked to perfection, and served by the butler and Hilary on the silver dishes bearing the Irving crest. The little round snowy table in the middle of the big crimson-hung dining-room, the shaded candle-light upon the silver vase of white orchids in the center, the "feel" of the large fine damask napkins across her knees, renewed in Sara the gentle cerebral intoxication she had experienced over the porcelain bath-tub in her dressing-room. After she had sipped half a glass of good claret, the color rose into her pale cheeks, her diamond eyes sent forth more brilliant rays, she talked dashingly of many themes, but said no more, that night, of advancing the day when women shall count all dross save the effort of her intellect to dominate slowly-awakening man.

When they returned to the drawing-room, she sat down at the piano and played so exquisitely as to finish the subjection of Marion.

"You must play for my father," cried the girl. "He loves music. If I could play like you, I believe he would have loved me," she added, with sudden pathos.

"You must make him honor your courage, your consistency," remarked Sara, her white fingers twinkling over the keys. "It is a great mistake for woman to suppose that she is dependent on man's love for her earthly happiness. Great Heaven! When one thinks how many things there are *besides* men! Are not we two, for instance, perfectly cheerful, comfortable, well entertained by each other? Why on earth should we hang our hopes and fears upon man's frowns and smiles, as most women do? A woman who has the world's applause, the world's indorsement, will she not often throw it all at the feet of some good-looking animal, and be wretched if he does not approve of her, and then crawl up like a spaniel to receive a pat of his hand? A girl like you who has brains, beauty, wealth, position, power to come and go, why should her life be blighted because the man nature has chanced to place in charge of her, unsolicited by her, refuses to smile on her unless she is the abject echo of his opinions?"

"Why, indeed?" exclaimed Marion, kindling.

"And, all said, what is man as we know him in our generation? I pass over the so-called man of the world, except to ask you if a season passes, in your society, when you don't see parents ready and willing and anxious to give their young daughters in marriage to the heroes with whose 'gallant' adventures the newspapers have been filled for years? Is there ever a time when you don't hear this rich bridegroom's gifts of jewels, and horses, houses, publicly extolled before other young girls as an incentive for them to go and do likewise, if they can? Let such things go. I speak particularly of the man of our homes, the average man we are called on to honor and obey. Is n't he a petty creature when you see him behind the scenes? A captious, whimsical being, unjust, and unwilling to admit himself in the wrong. Are his purpose, achievement, fair play, to be all devoted to outer affairs, and left down-town in his office, to hang behind the door there till he puts them on again next day? Why must he be wheedled — as God knows all women have to wheedle — in order to purchase peace at home? This is the cry of thousands of quiet home-keeping women, if they only dared voice it. This is one of the things we are trying to help them to speak out — and the time is coming when speak they surely will."

"Do you believe that all marriages end in this, if they end in nothing worse?" said Marion, with a shade of regret in her honest voice.

"My dear, if Asmodeus could lift the roofs of all the houses of all your acquaintances to-night, to jot down statistics of woman's dissatisfaction in his note-book, I 'm afraid there would be few from which he would go away carrying a blank page."

She struck into a bit of Chopin that might have been composed by Asmodeus on his return from such a statistical round as she described. Marion shivered, as if with cold, and Sara, jumping up, shut the lid of the pianoforte, abruptly.

"Come over to the fire," she said. "Do you mind my taking your tongs, and playing with your log? For so long I have dreamed of a wood-fire with liberty to poke at it unchecked."

"But, Sara, you have not answered me. Do you believe all marriage is a bar to the intellectual development of woman?"

"My dear, do you know what a Girton girl remarked not long ago? 'All might yet be well with us, if we could only have three generations of single women.'"

"I am not prepared to say that. I have too much tenderness for the memory of my mother." Marion looked over wistfully at an oil-painting of a pale, slender lady in a robe of velvet and sable fur, hanging upon the wall. "That was done by Cabanel from an old photograph some years ago, and my father thinks it very like her. She was an invalid, in charge of nurses, for years before she died; and I was not allowed to be much with her. But I remember certain expressions of her face when I came into the room — yearning expressions, as I now interpret them. She seemed to be wanting to save me from something that had overtaken her. The son she lost just before her own death was her joy and comfort. She had no fears of any kind for him."

"Do you not see?" exclaimed Sara. "She wanted you to be spared the inevitable disappointments of marriage and maternity. So long hovering on the threshold of another world, may not she have had power to see what was in store for a girl of your strength of character? She, I take it, was of a yielding character."

"Entirely so, I think. The gentlest, timidest, of women. I remember that when, just before she died, she called me to her, and said she had arranged, by

will, that I should have an independent income upon
reaching the age of twenty-five, she uttered the word
'independent' in a whisper, looking about her to see
that no one was in the room. And then she added:
'It is not that I do not feel your dear father will do
all that is just and best for you, my child. His judgment is so much better than mine that you lose little
in losing me. But perhaps you will marry, and there
are moments when every woman likes to feel she has
it in her power to supply her own needs — to give as
she likes. Since I have been married, your father
has been good enough to lift every care of my property from me. With my health, indeed, what could
he do, else? I have had only to sign the papers. But
you may not get such a husband as I have had, my
dear.' A nurse came in just then, and ordered me
away. I was a wide-eyed, serious child of twelve, and
my mother's words sank deep. Two days later, I saw
her again — in her coffin. After she was carried out
in it, my life went on with my new governess almost
as before. I scarcely missed my mother; but this
was not my fault."

"No, poor darling!" said Sara. "But I trust the
governess was able in some degree to supply her
place?"

"Miss Ainslie was an Englishwoman of the most
conventional pattern. She had brought up a Lady
Maud and a Lady Sylvia, so that my father congratu-
lated himself upon having secured her on her first
arrival to seek a far higher salary in New York than
her noble employers had given her in England. But
not knowing our customs in America, not allowing

3

for the impulse of revolt against authority in our air,
she made my life,— as I made hers, no doubt,— a
wretched one for six long years. A devotee to duty,
she never left me. I knew every one of her maxims
by heart. A-h-h! Do you wonder I rejoiced in going
to our college, where I expanded like a cellar-bred
plant in the sunshine?"

"And what became of Miss Ainslie?"

"Her father's death recalled her to England. I
have often wondered how she has adapted herself
to the new order of things over there — the new education for women, the university training, that was
to her like a red rag to a bull when I mentioned it,
here. She must be a much astonished woman."

"I am surprised your father consented to let you
come to us at Somerville."

"You could not have been more surprised than I
was. I was eighteen, just ready to go into society,
when Miss Ainslie quitted us. My father waked up
to confront that fact with genuine dismay. When he
was asked by my Uncle Joseph's wife if he meant to
give me a coming-out ball, or a reception, I wish you
could have seen his face. Then I took my courage in
both hands, and pleaded to be sent to Somerville. I
have always felt I owed the permission he granted to
my Aunt Joseph's offering to come over with her
girls, and arrange the details, and chaperon the affair
of my début."

"Your father, then, has an aversion to society?"

"Not at all. He is one of the men most sought
after for dinners, where, I am told, he is the life of
the table. Sometimes, when we dine out together,

I peep across at him between the lights and flowers, and wonder if he can be the same man I see, but don't dare interrupt by speaking to, behind his morning or evening newspaper. I am proud of his looks, of his wit, of his youth, for he is younger than most of his confrères — barely fifty now. Then I hope some other hostess will take pity on me, and invite me with him, so that I too can be charmed by him."

"I understand," said Sara, sympathetically.

"Oftentimes the older women of society say to me, 'What a lucky girl you are, to have that delightful creature to yourself!' I fancy what he would say if I told him he is called 'a delightful creature.'"

"And where, in this life you have been leading since you left Somerville, did the man come in to whom you have just ceased to be engaged?"

"Alec? I have known him always. Better since, after his graduation at the law-school, and a year of study in Germany, he became one of the 'juniors' in my father's law firm. For my father is in his first term, as you know, and has not been long upon the bench."

"I think I rather like your Mr. Alec Gordon," said Sara.

"I 'm sure I do. He is far and away the best friend I ever had. He understands me as well as a man can understand a woman. Not as you do, dear; that could not be. Intuition like yours is not born into man."

"It must have cost you something to give him up," said Sara, narrowing her diamond eyes after a little nearsighted fashion not unattractive.

"Yes. I wounded him. I disappointed him. For a time he will feel very sore. But, feeling as I do, I am not fit to marry. I can't tell at what moment I should say or do something that would turn him away from me completely. I had rather keep his friendship than ultimately lose his respect."

"It is too late to-night to discuss that most interesting question. I shall have to study you all before I can say whether I indorse your action thoroughly. But, after all, you should, at your age, be your own mistress."

"Yes; and on Saturday I come into uncontrolled possession of an income, not large according to values in New York, but a boon to me—three thousand dollars a year, left me, as I told you, by my mother."

"Three thousand dollars a year!" cried Sara Stauffer, sitting upright. "Not large? Oh! what could not I do with three thousand a year, safe, secure, coming in regularly? No struggle to pay rent, to pay board, to journey from place to place, to strain after new, whole clothes. Why, you who are cradled in eider-down have no conception what other women live on — what the world you are so anxious to go out and confront is to us who are at its mercy. Try to fancy yourself always, for instance, in one of those crowds going off a ferry-boat or pushing into the car of an elevated train. That's *my* world of every day!"

"It shall never be said, when I have the means, that I forget others less fortunate," answered Marion, simply.

"I am not afraid of you. Forgive my vehemence," said Sara, relapsing into her old pose. And so they

talked, till the fire on the andirons sank into the singing stage, and Madame Stauffer, gracefully covering
a tiny yawn, announced that she would like to go
to bed.

As they mounted the stairs, the butler, who had
just finished adjusting his master's little arrangements for a comfortable closing of the evening, came
out of the library.

"What a lovely room!" exclaimed Sara. "Might
I take one little peep?"

"I rarely go in," said Marion, while nervously preceding her friend across the threshold.

"Poor Fatima!" laughed Madame Stauffer. "I
believe if, after finding her predecessors hanging in a
gory row, she had had courage to face Bluebeard, and
threaten to report him to the police, there would have
been no need of the brothers riding up to deliver her.
In *our* version, if there are any deliverers, they shall
be sisters. Ah, what treasures of bindings! Now I
happen to know something about good bindings."

"What do you not know?" asked Marion, one ear
alert for her father's latch-key in the door below.

"I see we had better not stay. What if, some day,
he asks us to come in here and visit him?"

"He will never do that, Sara."

Sara was not so sure. Still, it was very well for
Miss Ainslie's pupil to preserve her illusions on this
as on many other subjects.

At this moment they both heard the click of the
latch-key in the lock of the front door.

"Shall we go up?" asked Marion, catching her
breath a little.

"Just as you like," her guest answered carelessly. As the two moved along the corridor, Judge Irving mounted the stairs. It seemed impossible that he should not have been aware of their presence, but he gave no sign — opening the library door, and retiring within, with the magisterial dignity of his usual movements.

"You do resemble him strongly," remarked Madame Stauffer, who, through those narrow, deep-fringed eyes of hers, managed to take in much of the fleeting show of life.

III

T was the witching hour of dinner at the Antediluvian Club. The tables in the dining-room were, for the most part, occupied. Men dining alone, in eclipse behind one or another of the favorite evening papers, eating or drinking intermittently the while, accounted for the disappearance from the reading-room of all the most desirable journals. Parties of two or three men — comfortable-looking bankers, brokers, lawyers, doctors, with snowy shirt-fronts and complexions of mantling red — laughed and jested together, making the most of their hours of good cheer, free from professional or financial cares. Here and there, sitting alone, might have been seen a man to whom neither the current tidings of the outer world nor the society of his fellows offered a surcease of the pressure of affairs. Upon his brow lingered the never-relaxing lines of worry. By and by his place will be found vacant, and the other men will read paragraphs announcing his death from apoplexy or heart-failure, or — if the struggle has been particularly long and fierce, and the disappointment crushing — by suicide.

Among these groups no trace was seen of the

familiar figure of "Johnny" Waters. Since time out of mind, this veteran had been a feature of the Antediluvian at its prandial function. He was a spare old bachelor, living, no one knew where or how —"over Chelsea way," some quidnunc, bolder than the rest, had ventured to assert.

Neither did any one know when Waters had possessed a new suit of clothes. He was, however, clean, if rusty, and his pocket, like the widow's cruse, was at no time entirely empty; it contained a few pieces of gold, which he had the habit of playing with, but never changed.

His diversions were an occasional game of billiards, pool, or cards, in which his adversaries were discreetly selected from among the feebler folk, who might be depended upon to pay the club-tax for the game, charged always to the player who loses.

An authority in gastronomy, the cooks and servants treated him with respect, the club frequenters bowed down to his dicta: and there was hardly a day when he did not dine well with and at the expense of somebody whose dinner he had ordered by special request. On occasions when an opportunity for this thrifty exchange of benefits did not present itself, Mr. Waters, after long waiting for an invitation, usually denied himself a dinner. Arriving at the club regularly at about five in the afternoon, it was his custom to order toast and a cup of tea—probably his first meal, so whispered the gossips, since the liberal repast overnight, superintended by him, and paid for by "the other fellow." As the dinner-hour drew near, and men, dropping in, went to the desk to inscribe their orders, he would be espied wandering about with a blameless expression of innocence upon his withered old face. What, then, more natural than that some would-be diner, assured of getting thereby the best the club contained, should ask "Johnny" if he were disengaged for dinner?

To-night, upon his absence the jokers chose to hang the time-honored story that he was either walking in the square below, engaged in buckling up his belt, or else eating macaroni in a cheap Italian restaurant. But the morrow would see him at his post, renewed in hope.

It was at the period of the repast when most men's orders had been served, that Mr. Robert Crouch — the opponent at billiards of Mr. Justice Irving — was wont to appear upon the scene.

Short, thick-set, breathing stertorously, with his waistcoat well exposed to view, his protruding eyes taking in the tables as he passed, Crouch had the offensive habit of slowly sauntering the length of the dining-room, scrutinizing every table, and gaging the social value of every man according to the dinner spread before him.

"Don't talk to me about him, sir," he had once observed regarding a local dignitary. "He's a pretender — a mere pretender. Why, when I met him just after he had ordered his dinner yesterday, and casually asked him what he was going to have, he said, 'Well, for one thing, woodcock.' And blame me, sir, if, when I passed up the room, I did n't see him in the corner pegging away at a blanked old prairie-chicken!"

Mr. Crouch, like Mr. Waters, did not object to being bidden to sit at the table of his friends. With all his bluster at the waiters, and all his braggadocio about living on the fat of the land, he was, when dining alone, generally observed to be attacking a slice from a joint, and a couple of baked potatoes.

To-night, having accomplished his customary espionage, and driven several quiet citizens to the length of a wish to strangle him for his impertinence, Mr. Crouch stopped before a table laid for two in the upper end of the room.

"Who 's due here, Clarkson?" he asked of that gentleman, just come in to take his own bit of fish and some chops at the adjoining table.

"Don't know, I 'm sure," answered Clarkson. "I 'm late myself; just stopped a minute to enter a line in the complaint-book about the disgusting way these waiters breathe into one's back hair. If a man happens to be bald, as I am, it makes him sneeze, by Jove!"

"What was the complaint yesterday?" said Crouch facetiously.

"Oh, I don't remember. Probably that the floor of that wretched library shakes so confoundedly I can't digest when I go in to read after dinner."

"Who is this table reserved for?" asked Crouch, beckoning the head waiter, who was not imposed upon by his large, authoritative manner.

"Mr. Gordon, sir," said the functionary, turning away at once.

"Alec Gordon? Who 's he going to dine, I wonder? Quite a spread, to judge from the forks and glasses!

Have you heard they are putting Gordon forward for United States Attorney, Clarkson?"

"Fact?" said Clarkson, with animation.

"Yes. They are working it up among them; and by Jove! sir, with the luck that chap has, I should n't in the least wonder if he gets it."

"I 'm for him, and here 's to his success," said Clarkson, draining his glass of claret. "But even Gordon's luck goes under, sometimes. His engagement with Marion Irving is off, by mutual agreement. I have n't the pleasure of knowing the young lady personally, but she 's a splendid creature to look at, and I condole with him over the loss of her."

"She 's no loss to a man in his senses," said Crouch, with a sardonic laugh. "Why, she 's daft, or nearly so, over 'women's rights'!"

"What extraordinary capers these females are up to, nowadays!" replied the cheerful Clarkson. "If you believe me, I got a notice from a committee of them, requesting me and 'all the *adult* members' of my 'household' to call somewhere to sign a petition to strike out of our State constitution the word *male* as a qualification for voters. Now, I have n't any household; but if I had, why should n't they ask my babies as well as my adults, if the thing is to put everybody on the same footing? Last year it was street-cleaning. All the pretty women went at you at dinners, and asked if you had influence with various 'bosses' whom they 'longed' to know. Well, they accomplished then what they set out to do, those charming creatures, I must confess; but why can't they rest on those laurels? The year before it was the abolition of ash-barrels. You could n't open your mouth to a girl at a party without having an ash-barrel thrust into it! They 've had their dab at city politics; and as to the Higher Education of Women, the University Settlement, and the Kindergarten Association, those we have alway with us — and we are allowed to buy tickets, or send checks for boxes for their entertainments, to an almost unlimited extent!"

"And Marion Irving is in the front rank of all this," put in Crouch, who did not relish having to listen to so long a disquisition. "What 's more, she 's got the Woman Question for a bee-in-her-bonnet, which lots of the others have n't. If I were Irving, I 'd lock that girl up, or send her traveling with a keeper; and, if he does n't do something of that kind, she 'll end by coming to no good."

"Hush!" said Clarkson, warningly; but it was too late. Gordon, accompanied by a blond-bearded, smiling young man who had something foreign in his aspect, was close upon them, and must have heard every word of the close of Crouch's speech.

A surge of anger came over Gordon's face. Wheeling quickly, he spoke in the offender's ear a few evidently stinging words, whereat Crouch, uncomfortably red, turned away, relieved by the coincident summons of a waiter to his modest meal served in a sequestered corner of the room.

"Ha! Clarkson," resumed Gordon, quietly, "I hope that cad has n't taken away your appetite. Come, after dinner, and let me make you known to my friend Baron Strémof, a Russian, just arrived."

"Charmed, my dear fellow, but what the deuce am I to speak in?" whispered Clarkson.

"English, of which he's a master," returned Gordon, going on to place his friend at table, and to introduce him to a plate of tiny oysters—a visible disappointment, as to size, for the new-comer.

"You had not—pardon me—a very agreeable moment in getting rid of the man who offended you," said Strémof, lightly. "But it was, at any rate, effectual. And these are the famed oysters—Blue Points, you call them. The flavor makes amends for their limited caliber."

"We reject the large ones, purposely, when served in this way. For once, you will find America not anxious to illustrate her excellence by size."

"Oh, you will not find me agreeing with any slur put upon America," said Strémof, with delightful animation. "It has been the ambition of my life to visit your country. And your Exposition at Chicago has made of last summer an ineffaceable dream of beauty to me. At even this distance of time the White City appears to me amid a luminous haze concealing all the petty vulgarity that must, of necessity, attend upon such a spectacle. I am more than ever lost in wonder at the fresh vigor of its conception, and the enormous abilities displayed in carrying it out. But I believe, already, you astonishing Americans are checking each other for allusion to the crowning glory of your age. A young woman of Chicago told me I must no longer speak of the Columbian Fair—that it is, by now, 'a chestnut.' Fancy! how delicious! I wrote home this little anecdote, and with it I am confident of amusing my friends in Petersburg. Would she consider St. Peter's of Rome, or St. Mark's of Venice, 'a chestnut,' may I ask?"

There was no venom in the lively strictures of Strémof, whose buoyant enjoyment of the world and of himself made him pleasant company. Everything interested him; nothing escaped him.

"If it has accomplished nothing else, the Fair has made us better known and understood by our friends from across the water," Gordon said. "And I think it has led them to understand, at last, that creation in art is possible to us."

"My dear friend," exclaimed the Russian, knocking over a glass of Sauterne in his enthusiasm, "who could fail to appreciate the fact that those splendid palaces of white 'staff'— built for a day, and already vanished into the fairy-land of dreams from which they came — typified the new birth of art from the virgin soil of America? What struck me most, after that, was the serious way in which the crowds, assembled to do it homage, received their impressions of your Fair. I thought those people from remote towns and villages, who had journeyed such immense distances, were especially interesting to watch. They seemed dazzled, oppressed, shy — but, through it all, proud and inspired. Henceforth, I thought, whatever they may read in their papers about the Old World, they will understand and enjoy. Some day they will bring their modernism to visit our antiquity — and, when they see our treasures, will not be ashamed because they have had nothing of that sort of their own. But here, as usual, I let my feelings run away with me. I *radote*, instead of doing justice to your menu."

"You say you have always had a wish to know us better," rejoined his host. "I can only regret you have put it off so long. Carroll's letter tells me you are amusing yourself by contributing studies, social and economical, of American affairs to some of your Russian journals. I wish I could enjoy them."

"I am indeed well protected by my language. But I am not afraid for any of my American friends to read them. They tell me, if anything, my letters are too uniformly *couleur de rose*. Yes, for some years before I came I had been gathering facts about you. Carroll, who is a charming fellow, and much liked in Petersburg, put me up to the books I must read to understand your social side. I wish you could have seen the bewilderment of an old countess with whom I go to take tea — who is by way of being an amateur in your literature — after I left with her a volume of American stories in dialect. 'But, my dear boy,' she said to me, 'as well expect my old teeth to crack nuts!'"

"And now," said Gordon, smiling, "I suppose you wish to find the originals of the types you have met in our novels."

"You have hit the mark! Here is my complaint — I have not met one of them. Where are they? In the ateliers of the writers, behind screens, supporting a mass of different costumes to be put on when the lay figure is required? Everybody I meet is conventional. I could do as well in London, Paris, Vienna, Rome, or by staying at home in Petersburg. Your clubs are superb, but the men in them are like those I see in such places abroad; your houses are little palaces, crowded with works of art. Your women, perpetually on the wing, sip sweets from the fashions and customs of every country to bring home. Even in the far cities of the West I found furniture and costumes and modes of living like these here, and all under the eternal glare of electricity. Imagine a continent full of New Yorks! Your men, more original in thought and expression than your women, are fast becoming super-civilized. I am in despair. If I could only meet on the street a lady — Bloomer, *c'est ça, n'est-ce pas ?* — in her trousers and pot-hat, I should be happier. But it seems to me that, even in London, the women are more fearless in action, in expression of opinion, than your women. I wish I could know an American unmarried woman of the sort I have dreamed of. I should not write about her in my notes for publication, *bien entendu*, but I should enshrine her in my heart."

"It would take me some time to explain to you the transition stage of society which is responsible for what you charge," said Gordon.

Strémof was silenced by his first introduction to terrapin. But not for long.

"This is wonderful!" he exclaimed. "I now confess to you, my friend, that it was with a species of resigned terror I tasted your national delicacy a moment since. Last year Carroll, who wished to make some acknowledgment of my father's friendship for him, ordered to be sent to our house, express from America, some terrapin in tins. I have since learned they had cooked and sealed it at the last moment before the fast steamer sailed, and had expedited it direct to Russia in the care of a friend, scarcely daring to hope it could arrive in good condition for immediate use. But my father, not understanding this, had his *maître d'hôtel* put the dainty away until the belated occasion of a dinner of ceremony to which Carroll was invited. The American dish came on; alas! it was left upon every plate! Poor dear Carroll, who did not in the least recognize it, had covered his portion with a piece of bread when he heard my father announcing to Count X—— upon his right that this was the famous terrapin of North America! My dear friend, let me thank you," he added radiantly, extending his hand, which the amused Gordon shook. "You have not only saved Carroll's reputation, but you have given me new bliss!"

Over their coffee, Clarkson joined them, and their merry talk was prolonged till Gordon hurried Strémof off to hear Calvé in " Carmen," and to make acquaintances in the boxes of a number of his friends. It so happened that, for this night, a woman inclined to be gracious to Marion Irving had sent a note inclosing three tickets, and urging Marion to join her in her box, bringing "any friends" she might select.

Marion, who had no taste for the conversational patter that accompanies the opera of to-day, had been about to decline the offer — when she saw in the eyes of Sara Stauffer an expression interpreted as a craving for the music so little within her possibilities.

"I could take tickets in the parquet, or in a gallery where it will be possible to listen in peace," said Marion; but a girl, happening in at the moment, as-

4

sured her of the impossibility of buying a seat for
Calvé in "Carmen" at that late hour.

"It is just possible Mrs. Romaine won't be in her
own box," she meditated; "if the fancy took her to
go to see Sandow the strong man, or the trained ani-
mals, she would follow it, and leave the box empty.
Yes, Sara, we will go."

Madame Stauffer, who had been waiting with a
strange palpitation of anxiety at the heart, looked
frankly delighted, and cried out with pleasure.

"I am hungering for opera," she went on. "But
oh, Marion, you know my wardrobe! What have I fit
to wear? There is a poor little white silk made long
ago for a concert of the graduating class at Somerville. Perhaps, if I bought a lot of that soft white
chiffon, and put it on in full ruffles around the
neck —"

"I think so," said Marion, absently; then, remembering herself, "Dear Sara, how vexatious it is that a
woman like you should be in the shackles of conventionality in dress. Why can't we soar out of these
petty considerations? You are charming in the little
black frock, with the black lace, and a red rose in
your bodice."

"To accomplish what we seek, we should never let
ourselves be remarked for singularity," said the teacher.
"Therefore, darling, as we are driving out, if you
will take me to some cheapish place to buy the
chiffon —"

Marion, obedient to a certain point, directed her
coachman to stop at the emporium where her own
purchases of that sort were made. A fichu of fine

white gauze, floating at a breath into a feathery mass, was found already made by skilled fingers, and was supplemented by new gloves of Sara's number, and the offer of a gift of Marion's best fan.

"How I rejoice in ordering these things to be charged to my own account," meditated the girl. "No more requests to step into the library to explain the items upon forgotten bills. But it surprises me that Sara should seem so glad to get them. I suppose it is only a refinement of the feeling she touched upon — her objection to illustrate Women's Rights by peculiarity of costume."

THEY were in the Romaines's box at the opera, alone, when Gordon came in to introduce Strémof. As Marion had predicted, the notional owner of the premises had elected to remain at home, or to go elsewhere.

Gordon, who, designedly, had not seen Marion since their rupture,— having gone off on business of his firm for a "little American journey" to Salt Lake City, and having but just returned,— observed her with surprise in the company of this peculiar but attractive-looking "woman in white," whom he could not remember having seen with her before.

For a moment he had hesitated in the lobby at the door of the box. Then, telling Strémof he was about to present him to a lady, young and unmarried, perhaps the best exponent among his acquaintances of the "unfettered American spirit" which Strémof aspired to meet, he opened the door into the anteroom.

Here, in the surrounding of crimson satin, decorated

with mirrors in Florentine gilt frames,—for Mrs. Romaine knew well how to set off her fading looks,—they found the two women, who had retired, during an *entr'acte*, from the glitter of the auditorium.

They were a pleasing contrast, nestling toward each other, as women sit, upon the crimson cushions of a little couch. Sara, dark, lithe, sparkling, all in white; Marion in satin, as usual, the color of her hair, with sleeves and scarf of a topaz yellow. Unconsciously, she had placed herself against her long coat of amber satin, with its many capes bordered with otter fur.

Strémof, the impressionist, seeing this artistic " composition," that might have been hung with effect on the line in the Salon of the Champ de Mars, was possessed with wonder that the two should be alone, when all the other women he had visited were subdividing their chitchat and attention between numerous male callers. He could hardly be expected to divine that it was the possession of the very independence of thought which he affected to be in search of that isolated the beautiful and distinguished Marion Irving from the class she belonged to.

When Gordon entered the box, Marion blushed, and then, feeling that the Higher Woman would not have done so, blushed again at having blushed. Sara, perceiving as much, understood, before his name was mentioned, who this great manly fellow was. Immediately falling into conversation with Gordon, she rose, and returned to the front of the box with him, followed by Marion and Strémof.

Sara's boast was not exactly like that of Wilkes, the most ill-favored Englishman of his day, who said that,

"THEY WERE A PLEASING CONTRAST."

with a half-hour's start, he would not be afraid of the handsomest man in the kingdom; but she knew how to value this opportunity to make a first impression upon her friend's friend.

Although he and Marion were no longer lovers, she had early realized the importance of Gordon's opinion to Marion, and to a more formidable power in the Irving household. She recognized that this strong, straightforward, clean-minded gentleman was not to be dealt with by any of the commonplace methods known to women who set themselves to attract men. She felt that he would not be easy to deceive. Her supple spirit, confronting his, yielded to it for a moment, leaving her almost at a loss. Then, rallying, she determined to compel him, before she was done with him, to admire her talents, enjoy her society, respect her. Ah! poor Sara!

After Gordon had talked with Madame Stauffer during a longer time than is generally allowed in a visit of the sort, he changed places with Strémof. The latter, finding Marion attractive, had yet been baffled by her odd reserve. He was rather relieved to plunge into a merry war of wits with her companion. With the foreigner, versed in such arts, Sara could let her rare facility in conversation have full swing. She flew lightly ahead of him, putting Strémof on his metal to keep up with her, and yet allowed him to perceive that he entertained her thoroughly. Like most strangers visiting America, he could not see the reason that, had he been an ordinary frequenter of New York society, would have made him give a cold shoulder to the little unknown woman who had no backing except Miss Irving's caprice in friendship. And there was one subject upon which they did not spar : Strémof, himself a brilliant musician, saw that in Sara he had met his match.

Thus, while their friends were in the stream of animated talk, Gordon and Marion profited by the first occasion for communication with each other since the breaking of their engagement. By the time he sat down by her she had regained her self-possession, and her glance, turned upon him, was full, free, and cordial.

" You have not told me how you like my friend ? " she said, dropping her voice, after a few generalities and a description of his journey.

" I have been patching together my recollections of what you have said about your acquaintances at Somerville, to try to place that rather dazzling person."

"In those days she was Sara Mills, a lecturer to our freshmen on English literature. After leaving Somerville she married a German professor, a Dr. Stauffer, as clever, apparently, as she; but the marriage was not happy, and he died very soon. I can't say that Sara, as I see her now, in the least suggests the little Miss Mills I first met. She is the most protean of creatures, and fascinates every one."

" How did you come to find her again ? "

" I saw in a woman's journal I subscribe for that she had been obliged to stop work from ill-health, and was in Washington ; so I wrote to her,"— here Marion colored a little at the recollection of the subject of that first letter,—" remembering her as the most sympathetic person I ever knew."

" It was a kind impulse to want to give her this

glimpse of brightness in her life. I can't imagine a more wretched breakdown than one from teaching."

"Oh, but I don't deserve credit for pure unselfishness," said Marion, always sensitively truthful. "I wanted her for myself. I wanted guidance in certain paths. I have not explained to you that for some time past she has been a public lecturer on the Woman Question, and has appeared on many platforms about the country."

"Good gracious!" said Gordon, with a jump.

"Oh, yes. And I am proud of her courage, and pluck, and talent. I think, as I know her better every day, I could follow anywhere she may lead. And, after all, it is to you I owe the permission to have her come. My father told me that you advised it in the first place."

"I—oh! yes, I did," said the unfortunate young man, remembering his conversation with the judge.

"But you did not know I was going to capture such a *rara avis*, did you? It is a great pride to me to show you such a champion of our Cause, one so fine, so intelligent, so truly a woman in all that is best."

"*Our* cause?" he repeated in a blundering attempt at an undertone that sounded like a groan.

"Don't speak so loud; you will be heard in the parquet," she said in smiling rebuke. "Yes, 'our Cause'; for I am quite decided, now. I mean to work for them with all my might and means when Sara shall have decided in what way it will be best."

"Your father?" said Gordon, helplessly.

"That is, of course, our greatest obstacle; though

Sara has won him over, in a way most surprising to me, to let her explain to him our aims and objects."

"Explain to *him*—" began Gordon, again, and stopped, feeling that he was not coming through this very brilliantly.

"Really, Alec, I never knew you so dull in taking an idea. Her logic, her reasoning faculties, would command any man's respect. There, the curtain is going up."

"May we stay a while longer?" he said, hating tremendously to leave her alone with his new foe.

"Certainly. We are deserted females, apparently. But when I have Sara to talk with, I never miss any one else."

Gordon, falling again into the chair behind hers, queried no more. The act progressed. Calvé had come upon the scene; and upon her the attention of the great audience was focalized.

There was the *patio* of the little *fonderia* in which *Don José* lounged upon the edge of the table, while saucy *Carmen*, a rose dropping from her dark hair, her glances as full of fire as were her motions of sinuous grace, swaggered before her lover's eyes, or danced and sang for him in a voice as rich as wine.

But of this Gordon saw nothing. Perhaps, under the spell of that lovely voice, the captivating sensuousness of Bizet's music, he was impelled to feel for the girl, so near him that his breath stirred the loose tendrils of hair upon her neck, a new awakening of the tenderness of their old relation; and then a vague alarm for her, the instinctive idea that she needed his protection, had greatly shaken his resolve to think of her only as a sister. Already, in the short time since she had thrown off his loving yoke, she seemed to have not only receded far from him, but to be quieter, more content, nay, happier, than while he had been pouring out on her the best passion of his young manhood.

When the *toreador* came on, and strutted his brief space before the footlights, and sang his familiar, ringing song, Gordon was glad of the burst of applause that followed it. He started from his reverie, uncertain whether he had uttered an actual sound; but as nobody seemed to notice him, he felt relieved, assured that he had not.

" Oh, my love, my love," he was saying within himself, " you did not kindle such a fire in my breast, you did not feed it all these months when I believed you mine, to have it go out suddenly at your bidding."

As *Escamillo* came back on his recall, the antechamber of the box was invaded by new arrivals; and at the close of the repeat, Mrs. Romaine and two others came to the front. The greetings and explanations that ensued effectually broke up sentiment; and, pledging himself to take Strémof to call at the Irvings's on the day but one following, Gordon and his friend took leave.

In the lobby he encountered no less a person than Mr. Justice Irving, hovering — rather uncertainly, it appeared to Gordon — around the door of the Romaines's box.

"I saw you looking after Marion, from the parquet," the judge explained hastily. "You know I never will spoil an evening of good music by sitting where people gabble, and Mrs. Romaine is notorious in that respect. She 's just gone in, I see; so that Marion 's all right. There 's no call for me to show in there, I suppose?"

"None, if it bores you, I should think," said Gordon, introducing Strémof.

"Then I 'd as well go back and get the rest of this act in my seat below," said his Honor, after extending a civil greeting to the stranger.

"May I see you on Sunday afternoon, alone?" said Gordon. "I am promising myself the pleasure of introducing Baron Strémof to your daughter on that occasion; and, if you are free, I will try for a talk with you."

"Of course, of course," answered the judge.

Then he hastened off; and Strémof had to repeat a remark he made to Gordon before it was heard, so intent was the young man in looking after the vanishing figure of his sometime father-in-law-elect.

"You are in a brown study," said Strémof, gaily. "Let me thank you for the delightful opportunity you have given me in that last visit. Now that we have left them, I see that, with all her sparkle, the *petite* Madame Stauffer is less remarkable than the young lady in her charge. One could readily commit folly for a Madame Stauffer, but any wise man would choose to live for Mademoiselle Irving. Why does not one of your American sculptors—your great St. Gaudens, for instance—see in her the new Pallas of the coming woman's era?"

Gordon, indisposed to talk on this subject, proposed

another call. As they threaded the half-circle of the lobby, various men, strolling outside, met them, and Strémof was quick to notice the tone and temper of the salutations bestowed on Gordon.

"You are like a hero returned," he said. "Every one welcomes you, and looks up to you. Pray, how long have you been out of town?"

"A fortnight," Gordon answered, and then wondered if that was indeed the length of time consumed by his journey. So much had happened since his departure, he felt that it must have been longer.

IV

RS. ROMAINE, who had never been beautiful, and was no longer young, brusquely cordial in manner to those she fancied, abominably rude to the people she chose to ignore, had a certain attraction of individuality that created for her a following of friends independent of her place and wealth.

Well-born, married to a prosperous and influential ruler of finance, she liked to take liberties with established things, which, when pushed too far, were usually atoned for by some entertainment from which society went away persuaded it could not have afforded to *stay* away.

On fairly good terms, as such things go, with her husband, she never failed to do herself the injustice of referring to him in public as an enemy of her peace, against whom her only protection was a series of needle-pointed sayings, repeated successively as "Mrs. Romaine's last." In actual fact, John Romaine—a man whose ambition it was to accumulate millions, to be panoplied with the world's adulation, to have his schemes and ventures discussed in the newspapers with the admiration for success that tempers, if it cannot subdue, the audacity of the American press — had come to care very little for what his wife did or said. Prosperity had driven them asunder, and their lives under the same roof were lived very much apart. Liberal to indulgence, Romaine enjoyed the dashing exhibition of his riches as dispensed by her hands. At the pace they were going, he had no time to wish her other than she was. He had no time either to regret the loss of his children in infancy, to wonder what he might have conferred upon posterity. The present, the great powerful present, rushing over steel rails with its iron wheels, in the glare of electric light, was his, and he exulted in his ownership, nor asked for more.

Mrs. Romaine, who, Marion thought, fancied the Irvings principally because they were so indifferent to her, now spoke to Marion in her usual sleepy, very-much-bored voice.

"Glad you could come, I'm sure. Isn't that the judge I see down in the parquet — that shocking man who never fails to snub me? We would have been here earlier, but on the way Reggy Poole was possessed with the idea of stopping to hear Lizzie Linwood sing, and we went in a box, just for the lark, you know. But she bawled, and I soon got tired. Who is the woman you've got with you to-night?" she ended, looking over at Sara, and hardly troubling herself to subdue her voice.

Marion explained.

"That alters the case," exclaimed the hostess, with animation. "She is talking to Reggy now, so in case I forget to mention it again, bring her to lunch with me to-morrow. Her subject, after socialism, is of all others the one that interests me now; if she's as clever as you say, why should n't we have an afternoon lecture for women, and let her 'give it' to the men? Poor creatures! I have a pet idea to promulgate, and perhaps I 'll start it, then. I want to open a kindergarten for husbands, who are nothing but children, morally, as we all know. We will set for them object lessons in consistency, and teach them how not to get out of responsibility crab-wise. You shall be a teacher, your friend chief lecturer, and Loulie Kemp, there, *might* have sense enough to distribute slates, and amuse the very little husbands who won't want to be taught. (Never mind! She don't hear me.) And what shall we do with Reggy Poole? I can't leave him out, can I, when he's always at my heels? Oh, he's so much like us, we 'd put a frock on him, and they 'd never know the difference. Now, say you 'll come to-morrow, my dear. I 'm *so* afraid it will go out of my head."

To the invitation thus extended Marion had very little idea of paying serious heed. But when, next day, after breakfast, which Sara and she had fallen into the habit of having in her morning-room, the matter was casually mentioned, she found her guest of another opinion.

"That woman is helter-skelter, foolish, strained, perhaps," Madame Stauffer said reflectively; "but she is at present with us, and we must use any weapon we can lay hands upon."

"Do you think so, dear?" Marion asked protestingly. "I had set aside to-day to send for some girls

I am sure you would be interested in, to come to lunch with us."

"And who are they, dear child?" asked Sara, sipping with satisfaction her cup of *café au lait*, her feet toasting on the brass fender before a blazing woodfire.

"They are well-born working-girls. One of them addresses envelopes and sends out cards for women of society; the other makes lamp-shades, and reticules, and cotillion favors. One has a drunken father who oppresses her; the other a young brother she is putting through college. Both have been successful, and deserve to be. They are refined, intelligent, cheerful, suggestive. I am never with them (they are friends, and constantly together) without coming away refreshed. Then there is a journalist, whose life is a perfect romance—I meant to ask her, too, on the chance of getting her; and a stenographer whom I know you would enjoy. These are the recruits I would choose for our army—not faded, whimsical women of fashion like Mrs. Romaine."

"But Mrs. Romaine has great wealth and power, you tell me. We need means for everything, beginning with the endowment of more colleges."

"New York is hardly the place to seek for that," said Marion, with kindling eyes. "Boston, New Orleans, and other places were before us in offering to women advantages in education approximating those enjoyed by men; and New York, the metropolis in point of population and wealth, has only now begun to move in that direction. If Mrs. Romaine and her set would take hold of that idea, and make it the fashion, it might be different. But they won't; they are not broad-minded enough, far-seeing enough; they do not altogether fancy dandling a cause which their men turn into ridicule. I 've seen it tried with them; you have n't. Believe me, by going to her you would only waste time, and sacrifice our aims as a toy for her passing amusement."

"But I think, my darling,"— and Marion had a dim sense that there was no use in trying to controvert one of Sara's "buts,"—"you must be content to leave some things to my judgment, without questioning it. I know that among us, in council, we have often wished for opportunities such as this seems to promise, to spread the doctrine; and I cannot, in conscience, abandon it."

"I only felt that a few words from you would mean so much to these earnest girls I spoke of," said Marion, submissively.

"It is a satisfaction to me to work in more difficult channels, once in a while," answered the reformer, preparing for herself, with great daintiness of touch, an orange. "For so long my efforts have been directed to showing the intelligent proletariat of the country the enormous mental, moral, and material gain that will come to them from woman's universal right to the ballot, it is time I should handle the class that is smothered in the eider-down of luxurious indifference."

"Mrs. Romaine *says* she is a socialist," said Marion, with a smile not repressed by the dignity of the subject.

"Better and better!" exclaimed Sara. "At last I

see the dawn of our opportunity. How I wish I could engage Mr. Gordon to let me explain to him our leading arguments, and hear some of his objections. Ah, my dear Marion, there is a man worth breaking lances with."

"I never broke any with him," answered Marion, half quizzically.

"I suppose not. He was a lover, out and out, I don't doubt; as he is everything he sets out to be— I am sure."

It is too recent for me to talk about, even to you," said Marion, confused.

"Very well, I shall respect your feeling. But one thing, Marion,"—and Madame Stauffer leaned over, and looked scrutinizingly into her friend's face,— "after meeting him last night, you are quite sure you do not waver?"

"I shall never be anything to him again, if that is what you mean," said Marion. "Even if I were made of the weak stuff to play fast and loose with a man's love, he is not the one to put up with it. He is still my friend—my best friend. I should hate to pain him by carrying out any scheme the Cause laid down for me that he did not approve of. But I should do it, nevertheless. I could never submit to the control that, as a husband, I felt convinced he would exercise over me. Every now and then, during our year's engagement, I used to come upon phases of his character that revealed this to me. My father says one secret of Alec's success in public life is his inborn power to rule men. His fearlessness of speech startles, but carries the judgment of others with it; his belief in

5

himself is infectious; his integrity is absolute—and his will sweeps over obstacles like a tidal wave."

To this Sara made a response that caused Marion to look at her in considerable surprise.

"A-a-h!" said the little woman, throwing her head back, half closing her eyes, and relaxing her slender body in her easy-chair. "If one dared let oneself go, what joy to be swept away by such a wave!" Then, sitting up erect, and dipping her fingers into her finger-bowl, she flicked the water from them into the air. "You look at me as though I were a mad woman, Marion. Perhaps I am, dear child; but, the truth is, when one has gone through my experience of battering around the world, there are moments of temptation to shut the eyes, and let somebody else fight one's battles—moments that come like the whispers of Apollyon to deter Christiana from following the right road. That's wretched femininity, I suppose—the weaker part we are all trying to live down. No matter! It's gone as it came. Such an indulgence makes me a traitor to my Cause. Give me my casque and doublet, Marion, and help me to buckle them in place."

Just then there was heard a tap on the door of the morning-room—a timid tap, a deprecating summons.

"Come in," said Marion.

The door opened, and upon its threshold appeared the judge, in his top-coat, holding his hat in his hand.

"Marion, my dear,—good morning, Madame Stauffer,"—he began, looking from his daughter to her guest, as if he had casually become aware of the existence of that lady — "I thought I would mention that I am engaged this evening at a meeting of our dining-club, from which I cannot very well get off, and it would probably be too late upon my return to hope for Madame Stauffer's assistance with my new catalogue of the French and Italian books in my collection. But if on Monday evening it would not trouble Madame Stauffer to resume her important coöperation —"

"You are too kind, dear Judge Irving," said Sara, "but Marion knows that is the day fixed for my return to Washington."

The words were commonplace, but the sigh that escaped with them was pregnant with pathetic meaning.

"Monday? Impossible!" said the judge, with a return of his imperative manner. "That is,"—he went on, as before,— "I don't know, of course, the engagements made for your valuable time, but I cannot suppose Marion has allowed you to feel that your visit to her has lasted long enough. As for me, I can only say that as long as you are willing to confer your — — er — inestimable companionship upon my daughter, I shall — er — consider myself your debtor."

"There, Sara!" said Marion, exultingly. "I told you papa feels as I do. We won't hear of your leaving us till after Christmas."

"What can I do but say yes, and thank you a thousand times?" cried Sara, dropping her eyes before those of the judge, while holding Marion's hand in her own. "This dear child, Judge Irving, is my sister of the heart; and you have made me so happy

in feeling that I can be of some little, little use to
you in your arduous brain labors."

The judge's ear was tickled by the phrase. He
loved to think of himself as a victim to over-exer-
cise of the mental faculties.

"It is—er—an immense gain to my work to have
from you such intelligent apprehension of its scope,"
he said, in rotund speech.

"And we are going on, also, with my attempt to
make you understand the real force and meaning
of the mission I am, however unworthily, trying to
sustain ?"

"Far be it from me," quoth the judge, "to wish to
raise a hand toward tearing down the veil of reticence
with which every shrinking woman should surround
her life before the public. But I concede what you
have said as to what they can accomplish in school
elections. More, I am hardly yet prepared to grant."

This concession, accorded with Jove-like dignity,
fell upon Marion's ears with startling effect.

"Ah! but if you will only have patience with me,"
said Sara, in her winning voice, "I shall not undertake
to alter your opinions—ah, no! That would be far
too much to aim for, too high an achievement in my
life. But I will dare to hope you may end by thinking that justice and honor might do worse things than
place in our hands the privilege of the ballot."

"We shall see; we shall see," said his honor, with an
attempt at amiability having rather the effect of a
grunt. But, as he bade them good morning and went
off to court, Marion thought she had rarely seen her
father wear such an animated expression of youth and

interest in current things. With a sigh, she said to herself, "It is his manner of society, of course, that makes all women tell me what a delightful man he is."

When he had gone, she dared not speak of this to Sara, lest that clever person should see farther behind the veil than Marion intended her to penetrate. Why should his own child expose his weakness? And Sara, equally discreet, said nothing on her side.

MRS. ROMAINE, doing the honors of her stately dining-room with careless grace, rather "laid herself out," thought Marion, to be civil and gracious to Madame Stauffer. The other guests at luncheon were Strémof, who at the moment of introduction the night before had been bidden by the hostess to come next day and make her better acquaintance; Miss Kemp, a colorless young woman serving to fill the vacant place in most of Mrs. Romaine's incomplete functions of life and society; and a pale, wild-eyed man dressed in threadbare clothes, who was introduced as "Herr Hofman, from Basel, a distinguished socialist," employed to come three times a week to "coach" Mrs. Romaine in the doctrines of his creed.

"Oh! you may smile," said the lady of the house to Strémof, who had treated himself to a small indulgence of the nature designated, "but until I had Hofman's talks, life was quite empty. I am so enthusiastic about it I mean to become a member of the American Branch of the League, shortly. Until then I must be content to give money—"

"They also must be content, madame," said Strémof.

"And to talk to any one I meet whom I think I

can influence. When I drive about to pay bills to
my tradespeople, I cast a seed here and there. I
have great hopes for an intelligent young plumber
who has lately been at work in the house; and "—
lowering her voice—"my butler and footmen are
hotfoot after the new doctrine."

"And so, when the day comes that is foretold by
Henry George," said Strémof, "which some one of
the Scotch writers has described as a 'huge wedge
driven through the middle of society, and on the un-
derside of it the merchant princes eating the bread
of poverty with their lowest dependents,' you are prepared to share all your present privileges?"

"There are some of my privileges I would not
only share, but give away with rapture," she said —
"the privilege of being bored to extinction by half
my acquaintances, for example. But we are not here
to talk about my 'mania,' as my husband pleasantly
calls it. Madame Stauffer must tell us of *her* mission, that I think should march hand in hand with
mine to the dawn of the New Day; and then Herr
Hofman may be induced to follow."

"Not at table, if you don't mind," said Sara in a
low, distinct voice. In her heart she resented the
airy impertinence of Mrs. Romaine's mocking manner, the fact that she had been brought there to
make entertainment, and was classed with the long-
haired man with a dingy shirt-collar.

"Has temper," decided Mrs. Romaine, internally;
then, turning away, she devoted herself to Strémof,
leaving the others to take care of themselves.

"For once," thought Marion, "one of her 'menagerie luncheons,' as she styles them, is a distinct failure."

And so it proved. The affair languished, until even Strémof, who had been making stupendous efforts to support the occasion, ceased to struggle, and went under.

"Goodness, how dull we are!" said the hostess, at last aware of the fact. "Let us go into the library, and smoke; and perhaps that will enliven us." And, rising abruptly, she led the way into a room where no vacancies appeared to mark the recent withdrawal from it of Mr. Romaine's treasures of books, now dispersed.

"My husband is bearing up under it as well as can be expected, thank you," she answered to Marion's inquiry as to how Mr. Romaine bore his loss of the famous library. "If there were a place to dispose of wives added to one's collection at vast expense, I suppose it would be my turn to go next. You know my husband does not illustrate — what Marx says, Herr Hofman — that 'the value of a commodity changes directly as the quantity, and inversely as the productive power, of the labor which realizes itself in that commodity.'"

"Ah, yes," rejoined her adviser, with entire solemnity; "you mean where he also says 'value is an immanent relation to socially necessary time of labor.'"

"This is not gay," remarked Strémof, *sotto voce* to Madame Stauffer. "Why should this lady, into whose cradle the good fairies seem to have poured all the gifts, be so sharp, so little restful? What a contrast to the old times when it was the chaplain or

father confessor who made part of the domestic staff
of the woman of place and fortune! Now she must
have her spiritual director in socialism, *mon Dieu!* Is
it so everywhere? Must I be ready on all sides to
talk of new doctrines, new ideas, casting behind me
the gossip, the pleasant nonsense, that is really the
high art of conversation? But, no, I will not ask that
of *you*, madame, since last night, when you gave me
a glimpse, all too short, of your own brilliant powers.
Tell me — and if I am indiscreet, silence me — about
that beautiful sphinx who is in your charge — Miss
Irving. She interests me. She perplexes me. Since
last night, when we parted, I have been trying to
solve her; but I do not succeed. Is she happy? Is
she sad? What is the secret of that noble expression of infinite patience upon her broad brow? You
smile — ah! I am always losing myself in my enthusiasms. But, I swear to you, for hours I have
thought of hardly anything but that girl, and have
dreamed of meeting her again. At table, to-day, she
surprised two or three looks from me that I could see
she did not fancy, and so I looked no more."

In a few words Sara told him the outline of Marion's
history, of her engagement to Gordon, and its ending.

"So?" said the young man. "And there is absolutely no chance that she will take Gordon back?"

"None," said Sara.

They were sitting apart in an alcove by a rack containing an open portfolio of etchings at which neither
looked. Strémof was struck with a certain expression
passing, like the shadow from a bird's wing, over the
speaker's face.

"Besides," she added, "Mr. Gordon is a man on the quick rise to power, to political fame. The world will soon afford him all the balm his spirit needs."

"He will be here presently," said Strémof, looking covertly at his watch. "We have an engagement to spend the afternoon together, to see some clubs and galleries, I believe; and he was not able to give the time to Mrs. Romaine for luncheon."

Simultaneously, a servant preceded into the room the subject of their conversation, on whose appearance Mrs. Romaine fairly clapped her hands.

"Now that you are come, we shall cease being at odds with one another," she exclaimed. "Here we are, a group of people, all clever and original — except Loulie Kemp and myself, who want to be made so. What better opportunity for something I have long desired — to hear Gordon's views on the Woman Question? And, to lead the way to it,— for no one believes more in fair play than I do,— will not Madame Stauffer open with just a résumé, so that all can understand our platform about the ballot, which is, after all, the main object of our hopes?"

At an ordinary time, no proposition could well have been more distasteful to Gordon. But he had parted from Marion, overnight, in a sort of blank terror as he thought of the gulf toward which, in his eyes, she was drifting. He knew she would never personally demand from him an expression of his views on the subject given. And he wanted to feel that, whether she recognized it or not, his hand had been stretched out to withhold her.

Sara Stauffer, on her side, was, as has been seen,

vexed and out of spirits. But, on Gordon's arrival,
her pulses had begun to stir with pleasure of the
most agitating and least welcome variety. It was,
indeed, a protest against her own infirmity of spirit
that spurred her on to enter the arena against the
young man who had so affected her. With eyes cast
down, with the hesitancy of a child, she began an exposition of certain arguments so well known of late
it were useless to rehearse them here. She gave a
brief history of the "disfranchised" classes of humanity, beginning with those in England, then passing to the negro, and finally to the women of the
States. The question of equal wages for equal labor
was next touched upon, Madame Stauffer making the
point that, until the power of the ballot shall be accorded to women, this equality cannot exist, and that
the first result of woman's "enfranchisement" will
be the opportunity to receive pay commensurate to
the value of her work.

She spoke simply, with an admirable choice of words,
with trained ease and rhetorical method, with convinc-
ing earnestness. The predominant feeling of her little audience, when she had finished, was one of respect
for the cause and the worker. Marion's heart swelled
with pride in her champion; and, stretching out her
hand to Sara, the two sat thus, while Gordon rubbed
up his wits for an answer.

"It is quite needless to tell you that I am tremendously at a disadvantage in this fray," he said
pleasantly.

"Madame Stauffer has brought the grace of her
oratory to the support of her, evidently, long-con-

sidered conviction. She has, of course, the sympathy, and deserves the applause, of her audience.

"I cannot, however, share her views on this subject; and — though I have never attempted a discussion of this kind, or any formal discussion in such presence, and must throw myself upon your considerate indulgence in entering at all upon a disputation before you, now, and so unexpectedly — I venture, in the rough, upon some of the ideas that occurred to me while Madame Stauffer was speaking.

"When the 'women's rights' insisted on by our agitators of the last generation related to questions of married women's property rights; or to the amelioration of the condition of women, to be afforded by laws more liberal in the matter of divorce; or to the authority a woman should have over her children — the right feeling and the good sense of the community were every year more and more with the champions of the sex. But in matters of divorce, any woman in this country can now be readily relieved of the yoke of a conjugal relation which ought to be dissolved for any substantial reason; the law among us is everywhere rather too lax than too stringent in that regard. Women have now been constituted by our legislature joint guardians with their husbands of their children — with equal powers, rights, and duties, in regard to their children, with their husbands; though I think experience will show *that* to be a measure open to the objection I shall presently make to female suffrage — that it tends to prevent a proper headship in the family. In the State of New York, too, the rights of a married woman to her earnings and in her property of every kind, acquired whether before or after marriage, are now securely established. Our statutes make her control of her real estate, for instance, more complete than a married man's dominion in lands held by him; in his lands she still has her right of dower. And in the other States of the Union those conditions have already been reached, or soon will be.

"The history of the growth and development of that legislation about the property of married women is, by the way, very interesting for this among other reasons. Our statutes on those subjects have revolutionized the law among English-speaking peoples everywhere. The first of them, in the States which began with the common law of England, was enacted in Mississippi in 1839. It was crude, but was amended and broadened in 1846, while the first of the New York statutes was not adopted until 1848; in fact, the Mississippi Act of 1839 was passed for special application to a particular case — was promoted by a bankrupt suitor of a prudent and well-advised woman, who had great expectations of estates she was unwilling to expose to claims by the creditors of an insolvent husband. To relieve the situation, the aspirant for the lady's hand had the bill put through the legislature, avowedly to introduce, not the rule of the civil law of Louisiana, which is enlightened in such particulars, but the tribal customs of the Chickasaw Indians, who were still numerous in the neighborhood! The squaw, as you may know, is the head of the family; the chief traces his descent, not from his father, but through his mother.

"But when the question of 'women's rights' has come to relate only to a demand that woman be allowed to vote at public elections, and upon questions affecting government and the State, it is a very different kind of thing, and seems to me to be but a symptom of the general drift of the age we live in, through socialism to anarchy."

At this point of Gordon's remarks Herr Hofman threw up his hands, with a resigned gesture, toward Mrs. Romaine, as who should say, "You see! As ever, we are misunderstood"; and Mrs. Romaine smiled back at him, consolingly.

"There never was, and never will be, government by all the people," went on the speaker. "Every form of government is necessarily more or less by representatives of the people. No system of government is or can be conducted by all the people by direct participation. Infants, for example, of either sex, are, like women, citizens — equally with men. But no one has ever proposed that infants be given the ballot to take part in actual administration of public affairs of the commonwealth. The line must be drawn somewhere between those who may exercise in person, and at the polls, the authority of a choice in prescribing the policies and designating the officers of government, and those who may not. The suffrage is not a natural right, like the right to life itself, but a privilege accorded by society to those members of the body politic who are thought likely so to exercise that privilege as to advance the general welfare in doing it—a privilege conferred, not for the special benefit of the individual to whom it is given, or in the interest of the class merely to which that individual belongs, but for the advantage of the Republic itself. When that franchise was allowed to the recently emancipated negroes of the South, for instance, so hazardous an experiment was justified, not as a present to the black for his own sake merely, but as an expedient, intended to be a means in his hands for usefulness to us all. For the good and peace and prosperity of the whole country, it was considered wise to intrust to those who had been slaves a weapon of protection against the possible oppression of so numerous a class, left otherwise very much at the mercy of a reckless or resentful body of their former owners, who, unless held in check by the ballot, which could choose legislatures and executive officers of government, might indulge in practices destructive to the best interests of the nation,—of the residents in New England as well as of residents in Carolina,— practices inviting to civil strife, violence, and insurrection, as well as to other occasions for a general disturbance of the well-being of society. And we cannot even deal, in this matter, with women as a class by themselves; they have, and can have, no interests, as women and as a class, conflicting with, or different from, the interests of their husbands, fathers, brothers, and sons, as men and as another class. There are classes among women, as there are classes among men: but surely men and women are together and united in every interest which concerns the welfare of the community as a whole.

"It is, therefore, not true that by withholding from women the authority to vote in person they are deprived of a right, or denied their proper influence in administration—any more than it can be said that because, not being a senator or a representative in the Congress, I myself am not allowed to vote upon the passage of bills pending at Washington, I am deprived of a right to a voice in government. Though I never vote in person, in the House or in the Senate, I do vote there, every day, by my representative.

"The unit of the social state, to be considered in such a matter as this, is not the individual, but the family; and things that tend to develop and maintain well-ordered and harmonious families should be the first care of the Republic. Women, at every election, vote by their representatives who, in any properly constituted domestic relation, feel, and respond to, and act under, the due influence of their womenkind in everything the latter are interested in."

"Pardon me, but is n't that more Utopian than Herr Hofman's vision of a new world under socialism?" said Mrs. Romaine, in her provoking little drawl. "But pray go on, Mr. Gordon. I am so glad to know that John Romaine is always thinking of me, at the polls."

"I have just reached the special point I desired to make," Gordon resumed, with a smile. "In every government, whether of the State or of the household, there must be one head, or there will always be confusion. There are many individuals who now enjoy and exercise the electoral franchise whose participation in government could be dispensed with, to the advantage of the country. There are cases where the wife is the real head of the household, and where it would be better if the law recognized and dealt with her as such, and allowed her to exercise all the power of such a situation. But laws are rules of conduct provided, not for exceptional cases, but for all; and, constituted as human nature is, society, the world over and in all ages since we emerged from savagery, has found that, as a rule, the man must be the head of the family. With understanding between them, the wife has a fit representative in her husband in the matter of voting. And where they differ so strongly as to make it useful to her as an individual, perhaps, to have her destroy his vote by voting against him, it is, in another and more serious aspect, and *as a rule*, a source of danger to the community to allow her the opportunity to do so. It would foment discord in every household where the husband and wife disagree, to confer upon woman the right to vote; all domestic headship and authority would be subverted. And when there is no longer a government in the households—the homes—of the land, there may soon be a subversion of all government; and anarchy will then have come."

When Gordon stopped speaking, he did not venture to look directly at Marion. He felt rather than saw her exchange glances with Sara Stauffer, who, with great tact, good-humor, and cleverness set herself to refute his argument.

Whether she did so to her own satisfaction, she was greatly applauded; and the hall-clock, striking four, broke up a sitting prolonged beyond expectation of any of them.

"How admirably she speaks! How well she has

herself in hand!" Strémof remarked to Mrs. Romaine, as he was taking leave.

"I belong to a club of women," said the hostess, "who meet from time to time to discuss current topics of thought; and I assure you that, among them, Madame Stauffer would be only incidental, not phenomenal."

"Is Mademoiselle Irving among them?" asked the Russian, whose eyes had been wandering more than was good for him to the tall girl in the black serge costume, sitting in such immovable earnestness through it all.

"She? Oh, no. We are not quite intense enough for her. Because I give dinners, and go to balls,— and spar with my husband, religiously,— Miss Irving thinks I have no place in serious thought. Good-by! So glad you were not bored by our impromptu duel. Sunday afternoons, remember! And you will let me send you a ticket for my box at the opera on Wednesday?"

"DID you tell me you had never met this Madame Stauffer until last evening, when I did?" Strémof asked Gordon, as the two men got into their hansom at the door.

"Never."

"And may I venture to ask whether you did not, until then, know of her relation to Miss Irving?"

"They were friends in Miss Irving's college-days, but they have not met in years."

"Well, my dear friend, if you will permit me, I must felicitate you upon a conquest," said Strémof,

C

gaily. "The little lady asks nothing better than to test, through you, the practical value of a head to her household."

"Absurd!" said Gordon. "Don't make me feel any more of an ass than I already do, after holding forth seriously on that theme in a drawing-room."

"But you did not convince Miss Irving," went on the audacious fellow. "Her face, as I watched it, was cold; her eye shone clear as polished steel."

"This club where we shall next stop—" began Gordon in a manner that admitted of no further trifling; and on he went, to fulfil his duty of cicerone, with a description that was cut short only by the stopping of the cab.

 GOOD Briton, says Henley, must wear his heart in his breeches-pocket, or anywhere but on his sleeve. Alec Gordon, a good American, did not consign to his breeches-pocket the heart so unceremoniously returned to him by the girl he loved, although he certainly did not wear it upon his sleeve. He put it, rather, into an office envelop stamped with the firm's name, tied it with legal tape, and consigned it to a pigeon-hole of his desk. There was work in plenty, and of a congenial sort, ahead of him, without forever playing the lorn lover. When he awoke on a bright, crisp Sunday morning, the day following his meeting with Marion at Mrs. Romaine's luncheon, and went to his window to fill his lungs with invigorating air, he felt that delight in living, that renewal of mind and body after healthy sleep, which is nearest akin to being born again in the flesh.

A church-bell, sounding near, did not act upon him like a prick of conscience, as it does upon older people who have nearly lived their span. He liked its reminder of peace and order in the calm of the usually noisy streets, as he did the Puritan demureness of many of the groups trooping churchward, and the quiet space to think and be glad in his youth and strength. Through his veins ran an exulting sense that the world outside his narrow chamber was his heritage, where there was nothing seriously awry in which he might not take a hand for bettering it.

But while, in bright day, the image of his lost love may not have glowed as effectively as in the mystery of night, when others around it had faded, his loyalty to her and to her father remained undiminished. He was not satisfied with the new inmate of their home. The hold Sara Stauffer had evidently acquired there made him vaguely uncomfortable. That afternoon he should make it his business to warn the judge in plain words that his daughter's friend was an unsafe guide for a girl full of opinions, like tendrils swaying in the wind, seeking a support to cling to. Disagreeable as this task might be, it was rendered doubly obligatory upon him by the fact that from him had originally come the urgent request that a companion to Marion's solitude be provided according to her wish.

Strengthened in disagreeable resolution by bath and toilet and a cup of tea, he stopped, on his way out of the building, at the quarters of his friend Clarkson. Of this gentleman he caught a glimpse in his inner room, in light attire, engaged in a matinal exercise of lifting himself some hundreds of times successfully upon his toes, with a view to the ultimate enlargement of a pair of unsatisfying calves.

"Sit down, old chap," called out Clarkson, cheerfully. "I'm on my last hundred, and shall be with you in a minute — ninety-four, ninety-five, ninety-six — I'm really tremendously encouraged. Talk about climbing Alps — ninety-seven, ninety-eight — it 's nothing to this — ninety-nine, one hundred — there! I really believe I'll be able to wear knickerbockers this summer. Though the increase in girth is slow, I don't find the exercise half so tiresome as I did, and I mean to give the thing full trial. Stop and breakfast with me, won't you? Can't promise you much to eat; but I'll have my tea and toast and an egg in, directly."

"It is so late now, I 'm going to lunch with my maiden aunts, instead of breakfasting," said Gordon. "There 's a matter I want to consult you about. I think you told me you have a relative who was or is one of the instructors at Somerville College?"

"Yes," said Clarkson, emerging in a gorgeous dressing-gown. "A cousin — about my age — brought up in our house. Don't mind telling you that I 'd have married her once, if she 'd have had me. But she preferred single-blessedness, and illimitable power to boss. Nice little fortune of her own, too. Teaches because she likes it. Writes pamphlets — all that sort of thing. Fine woman, though — very."

"Could I trouble you to find out from her, in confidence, any information they may have in the faculty about a lady who was once an inmate of their institution?"

"Gad! you speak as if it were a lunatic asylum, Gordon," said Clarkson, with a grin. "What you mean is a 'student at their university.'"

"Not a student — a teacher," said Gordon, giving
the name of the object of his search.

"A client, eh?"

"I am acting in the interest of a friend; and I
need not tell you that whatever information I receive
will be treated with respect, and brought to bear only
upon righteous ends."

"I 'll write to Kitty to-day — Katharine — I beg
her pardon. And to think, Gordon, that woman —
nicest creature you ever saw — round and rosy, with
dimples — by George! such dimples! — might have
been my wife long ago, if she had n't sacrificed us
both to an ideal. Said I would n't sympathize with
her aims, and therefore she could n't make me happy.
Here I am, an old bach.; and she a spinster of thirty-
five — pretty still! Well, hearts don't break, Gordon; hearts *don't* break, in this world. Look at that
for a pair of calves, now. Pretty fair, are n't they?
Not quite up to silk fleshings for a fancy ball, perhaps — but fair. I 'm thinking of going in for a new
health-food I 've seen greatly advertised for fatten-
ing, if I could be sure of getting it properly cooked
at the club. That 's one advantage a man has when
he 's married, Gordon. He can keep at it till they
cook things to suit him in his home; but the nui-
sance of trying to teach those servants at the club
is — why, sir, I —"

"I won't keep you from your breakfast, longer,"
said Gordon, smiling. "Good-by, and thank you for
your promised coöperation in my little affair."

"Little affair," he repeated to himself on his way
to luncheon with his aunts. "That 's a misnomer.

Marion's life, heretofore, has been like a fair white page. What may not that woman inscribe on it? For I do not, I cannot, feel satisfied there is not a niche sealed up in Madame Stauffer's past, that contains some record of a moral warfare with society in which she has been worsted. She is a mistress in the art of self-control, but I saw in her eyes that which sought to evade the too close scrutiny of mine. It was but for an instant, but the red flag warned me; and for Marion's sake, I pray God the woman may be got out of Marion's home and thoughts as quickly as possible."

THE Misses Stella, Clarissa, and Euphemia Gordon enjoyed the claim to respectful consideration, rare in New York of the present day, of residing in the house where they, and there father before them, had first seen the light.

Now well advanced in years, these maidens, whose fortune was to descend to the son of their younger brother Alexander, had survived the old-time pretension of the family to "lead New York." From time to time, indeed, they received their friends in this. house built by their grandfather on a suburban property of his near the Hudson River, in preference to a site of greater value in Broadway, because the old gentleman feared the noise and dust of a post-road outside the windows of his wife's drawing-room. On such occasions—although fashion, save when engaged in paying its respects to the Gordons, had kept aloof from the spot now hemmed in by houses given over as tenements to an encroaching popula-

tion of foreigners, its garden overshadowed by an
elevated railway—" every one" was there, because
not to be seen there would have argued unacquain-
tance with the " best old stock."

New-comers and youngsters of the ruling generation might stray through the large, dull rooms, wondering how life could have been endured upon carpets
artlessly sprinkled with the lily and the rose, amid
furnishings of rosewood and satin damask, giran-
doles with twinkling lusters, florid mirror-frames,
and statuettes on pedestals in every other window.
But still society respected the Gordon house, and
obeyed its summons as of yore. In the eyes of some
ancients there lingered about the place a softly lam-
bent halo, recalling the merry days of their youth.
It was all very well, they would allege, for brilliant
latter-day architects to reproduce, for new people
with long purses, purely "colonial" interiors, and
call them a revival of the best of early American art.
Early America never dreamed of such beauty and
harmony as these artists evolve for their clients.
But, with all its sins against modern creeds in deco-
ration, here were the actual surroundings of the gen-
tlefolk who were the founders of their body social.
One must needs be a Gordon to display now, on a
center-table with a marble top, a wreath of shell-
flowers under a dome of glass.

As far as Alec knew, this wreath had never left
this table. So, also, on a little mahogany stand in
the dining-room, a "Scott's Bible" still nestled in a
worsted mat. This he could not see without a vision
of himself in infancy at family prayers, fatally im-

pelled by original sin to kneel where he could have an eye upon a certain china basket containing crullers, kept always upon the buffet. Abhorring at this date of his life the old Dutch dainty as he had loved it then, it was yet inextricably associated in his mind with the act of devotion.

Through a like twist of psychology, he could never kiss the ivory-tinted cheek of his Aunt Stella, presented to him by that gentle old lady, without fancying he perceived the scent of rose geranium in the air. He had always heard of her "dressed for a party" in a book-muslin, with a blue scarf, a cameo brooch, a camellia with rose-geranium leaves in the hair behind her ear. This tradition of the family beauty equipped for conquest, as described to him in childhood, was indelible; as likewise the picture of Aunt Clarissa dancing a shawl dance for the company at a ball given upon her "coming out." Alec quite believed he had seen the latter performance, although a reflection upon dates would have proved it impossible.

The same endurance of early impressions upon the mind of a child kept in him a faint belief in the ability of puzzle-cards tied together with faded ribbon to amuse a visitor. Nor did he doubt that Aunt Clarissa had an "admirable finger" for the guitar; and he sympathized earnestly when Aunt Stella confided to him that, in deference to a promise once extracted by her mama, she had never read any of the works of Lord Byron!

His two elder aunts, who were twins, were sitting together awaiting summons to the early dinner that on Sunday did duty for luncheon, when Gordon was shown into their presence.

The dim room, its shutters bowed to keep sunshine from the carpet, the gray cerements upon chairs and sofas, the tiny coal-fire in the grate, Miss Stella's pug, and Miss Clarissa's pussy, were all as usual.

The sisters, having returned from morning service, were, according to custom, engaged in analyzing the sermon until the dinner-bell should ring.

As the young man entered, Aunt Stella arose automatically and presented her cheek for his salute. Alec knew just how many steps he would have to make across the hearth-rug to meet Aunt Clarissa and *her* cheek. Then, sitting between them, he heard from Aunt Stella the exact condition of Aunt Clarissa's health, and from Aunt Clarissa how the last medicine had affected Aunt Stella's harmless malady. It was next in order to stroke the cat, which, advancing to greet him, made of her back an arch against his leg, and the pug, which, resting his forefeet on Gordon's knee, wheezed an asthmatic "how d' ye do."

"And Aunt Effie?" asked Alec, cheerfully.

Aunt Stella cleared her throat in a feebly deprecating fashion. Aunt Clarissa did likewise.

"Euphemia has not yet returned from service," said the twins, reluctantly.

"She still keeps up her preaching to those poor people in the Hell's Kitchen district?"

"Oh, yes, my dear Alexander; she still does," said Aunt Stella, the readier speaker of the two. "When I think of my poor mama, who was the most shrinking and sensitive of females, of my papa, who had a horror of ladies of our position being put before the public in any way — I really am almost glad they are spared Euphemia's extraordinary conduct. To teach in a Sunday-school — that, indeed, is one thing; but to conduct a service of her own arrangement,— a service *not in the prayer-book*,— to stand on a platform and speak before the men and women of that horrible quarter!"

"Yes, my dear Alexander, in spite of all we can say," chimed in Aunt Clarissa. "It is not only that she has the most shocking-looking characters calling here and waiting in the hall; that she receives visits from people who, I know, had just as soon as not throw a bomb into our dining-room if they caught a glimpse of the plate upon the side-board; that she attends meetings, and offers resolutions just like a man: but she now writes for the newspapers — and what is going to become of us, Heaven knows!"

"At Effie's age, she should be more careful than she is of appearances," began Miss Stella; "not even a maid to attend her when she goes into those dreadful places!"

"At fifty-odd I think Aunt Effie might be trusted," said Alec, smiling; and the midday meal being announced, his energies were for a time devoted to carving a turkey upon a willow-pattern dish, and to appeasing the pangs of his vigorous appetite.

"What has Aunt Effie been writing about to the newspapers?" he said, at a convenient opportunity.

"Hush!" said Aunt Stella, warningly, till assured that the servant was out of hearing. "We try to keep it from our people, Alexander. It is a great

sorrow, but we must bear it as we can. It was bad
enough when she wrote a letter defending a Greek
flower-seller unjustly arrested, and even went into
court to testify to his good character; but what will
you say to her communicating to the press a new
scheme she has for the cremation of — I hate to mention it at table — of — garbage in the flats of poor
people ? "

"Kitchen refuse would have been a better word,
sister," said Clarissa, in mild rebuke. "Yes! What
a subject for a refined, elegant female. Why, she
should not know that such a thing exists!"

"It is a mystery I can never solve, why Euphemia,
who was given just the advantages we had, should
be so far from sharing our tastes and occupations."

"Alec, my lad, you 're as welcome as flowers in
March," exclaimed a hearty voice; and Miss Euphemia Gordon, in a tailor-made suit of masculine cut,
and a pointed felt hat, walked into the dining-room,
and took her place, after greeting her nephew with a
stout shake of the hand.

Between the pastel tints and old-time poses of her
sisters, this daughter of the house of Gordon resem-
bled a vigorous sketch in black and white. Stout of
frame, and never in her best days called handsome,
Miss Effie's face was radiant with health, good-nature,
and indomitable purpose.

Luncheon over, she carried Alec away to her own
room, an apartment severely devoted to papers, a
table with a type-writer between two southern windows full of sunshine, some chairs, and a desk, of
which the pigeon-holes were well filled with neatly

parceled documents. Here Miss Effie transacted the business of her life — in its broadest and truest sense the business of other people's lives.

"Now, answer me," she asked, wasting no words in preliminaries, "what did you mean by going off on that journey without coming to tell me in person of your trouble with Marion?"

"I simply could not speak of it," he said.

"I ought by this time to know the Gordon lock-jaw," she said, sitting down in her office-chair, opposite him. "Well, are you disposed to be more communicative now?"

"I ought to hold you accountable, Aunt Effie," he answered, with a half smile. "It is your creed that has infected her. And all this while I was comforting myself with the idea that, if Marion's indulgence in certain notions should make her turn out to be such a big-souled woman, helpful to herself and all around her, as you are, they could do her only good."

While he told her in brief his story, Miss Effie, listening, let the tenderness of her nature creep into her homely face.

"My boy," she said softly, when he had done, "don't you know we women have to learn our wisdom as you men do — by experiments, blunders, and new experiments controlled by experience? And don't you know my ideal society, wherein men and women shall work side by side, having share and share alike of the duties, responsibilities, and rewards of life? I had hoped that you and Marion were going to be its corner-stones; and if she has stumbled and fallen away from you in the darkness before dawn, I mean to believe that you will grope till you find each other's hands again, and grasp them never to be separated."

"I 'm afraid you 're a dreamer, dear Aunt Effie," the young man said sadly.

"It 's the first time I 've been accused of it then. Bless me, Alec, don't I *know* this girl is just stifled by the life she 's been leading as a polite slave of the nineteenth century in America. She must have time and opportunity to gratify her longing for a certain independence of thought and action; to find out for herself the values of the prizes of life, before she settles down to the task of being a wife and mother. She can't compromise with her conscience, to sacrifice to the petty duties of home her mental powers, until she has tested the exercise of them in a wider field. You ask me what she wants to do — what she thinks she can do? You don't know, I don't know; perhaps she does n't know yet. But she has put to herself the question that is the question of the age: 'What am I? What do I mean to be? Am I not folding my talent in a napkin, by just allowing a man to love me and loving him in return? Who knows how long this love will last intact? When I look around me, what do I see but strained, disillusioned couples, who live together because they have sworn to do so, whose hearts are cold, whose spirits hold each other forever to account?' Marion may not recognize this, but it is what makes her fearful. The sense of her responsibility to herself is just now greater than her desire for love."

"Decidedly greater," said the young man, with a reddening face, as he got up to walk about the room.

"Now, Alec, don't be miffed with your plain-speaking old aunty. If Marion knew you as I do, she would have no fear. Be fair; and own that if all girls weighed as well their chances of married happiness, there would be fewer of the fearful mistakes we see about us. But no! Most of them go to the altar, their heads dizzy with their own importance, with thoughts of their presents, bridesmaids, jewels, establishment, at the side of a lover who swears they are perfection. How many of these escape the hour of bewildered dismay when they realize the bond that makes them subject for life to a man they can have known only on the surface? I believe if wedding-presents could be made into a pile, and the wife of a month could offer herself upon them in suttee, it would be a not uncommon event."

"You are not cheering, Aunt Effie."

"But I speak the truth — the truth that mothers know, and yet hide under wedding frippery, giving their girls no chance to discover it, until too late. It seems to me that, until girls are educated to think and act more freely, even the foreign fashion of the parents deciding for them in marriage would be a wiser one than that now prevailing."

"No fault can be found with the average young woman's willingness to 'know all things,'" said Gordon. "That is, if we are to judge by the freedom of speech and discussion that seems to be the outcome of young woman's emancipation. I declare to you, Aunt Effie, my gorge rises at the books I hear discussed in modern drawing-rooms. I am told even school-girls read these stories, written by women 'with a purpose,' happily sometimes too well-veiled to be perceived by their innocent readers. But who knows, if they are to explore all veins of thought, what our girls will not come to knowing or surmising? No, no; the girl of my imagination, like that of every honest and healthy-minded young man, is the old-fashioned Una sitting upon the lion's back, passing unsmirched through the world—the girl who loves and trusts, and accepts with womanly dignity the lot her Creator has set aside for her. As to some of the advisers of young femininity in these days—those who rant and shriek, and ferment society without arriving at any result—may the Lord settle with them according to their deserts for the mischief they are doing!"

"I don't know what they are reading, and I don't go to the play," said Miss Effie. "When I want to be entertained I just take down a volume of Sir Walter Scott, or Thackeray, or Dumas. I feel no call to investigate these Ibsens and Maeterlincks, and the queer English novels—written generally by women, as you say—I see mentioned in the newspapers."

"I wish there were more like you, Aunt Effie, and you might bring us over to your way of thinking."

"Oh, my dear, I am just a plain old woman, not clever or progressive, in the 'highfalutin' modern sense. Long ago I found out my work, and I am happy without husband or chick or child. I have never had experience of the feverish mental conditions of many women of this hour—but I can understand them, and, in a degree, sympathize with them. I believe they will end in something sane and sound. And, to come back to where we started,—to Mar-

ion,—I repeat that she is developing in a period
when women no longer accept their fate blindly.
She knows it would be as disastrous to you both, to
devote her life to a union in which she is not absolutely sure of her willingness to submit to a tremendous will like yours, as to live that life in any mere
self-indulgence."

"Marion could hardly have felt herself called on
to sacrifice anything that is good in her to selfish or
trivial demands from me," he said coldly.

"There, there, I 've cut you, without intending it.
I know you, but how can she? How can any girl
know the lover who is captive to her youth and
beauty? She sees you through a veil, dimly. Bide
your time, and I trust she will come back to you —
for, oh, Alec! what a grand couple you would make!"

Aunt Effie's all-feminine burst of admiring cham-
pionship was too much for her nephew's sense of
humor. He laughed; she laughed, patted his head,
made him light a fresh cigar; and, stretched upon
her hard little lounge, he entered into one of the
long, intimate talks he well knew how to value.

LATER that afternoon Gordon met Strémof, and
took him to the Irvings' house. They found Marion
in the drawing-room, who told them that Madame
Stauffer, having letters to finish, would join them
before long.

Then Gordon, seeing Strémof's anxiety for a conversation with Miss Irving in which he might not
be always a third between two people so linked by
past relation, took the opportunity to seek the in-

7

terview with Marion's father to which he was urged
by conscience rather than by inclination. There was
no false sentiment in his mind about ousting the
homeless little person safely ensconced in Marion's
chamber, in possession of all the privileges of Marion's dwelling. If she were, as he honestly believed,
dangerous to Marion's peace, then go she must. And
yet he wished it could have been another than himself who was to sow the seed of doubt of her in the
judge's unsuspecting mind.

Thus pricked by regret, he opened the door of the
library—a spot where he had never failed to find the
warmest welcome; and there saw what intensified
his original mistrust.

In his great arm-chair, his hands folded, leaning
back with a look of entire mental satisfaction, sat the
handsome judge, over whose fine, clear-cut features
the firelight played with cheering warmth. At the
end of the table nearest him, Sara Stauffer, pencil in
hand, was checking off a catalogue of an expected
sale of books, writing upon the margin notes at the
dictation of his Honor.

Gordon well knew the task. It was one in which
he had often served the judge as Madame Stauffer
was now serving him. Judge Irving had no instinct
of the solitary bookworm who burrows in the dark.
He liked to discuss, with some confidential and ap-
preciative spirit, values, editions, bindings, the question of duplicates of the volumes he desired. Once
acquired, the books were apt to remain upon their
shelves, unless taken down for dusting or to display
to envying connoisseurs.

It was not the service yielded by Sara Stauffer that made Gordon conscious of a stab of disagreeable surprise. That might have been exacted by the judge from any one intelligent enough to render it, and tactful enough to make him think all the wisdom in the matter came from him. In the curves at the corners of the judge's lips Gordon could read vanity well satisfied by daintiest feeding. After all, what could a dependent creature like this do better, to make herself welcome in a house where a guest stopping over night had been till now a thing almost unknown? No, it was not the subtle incense which Sara had been burning under the judge's nostrils that Gordon objected to. If poor Marion had burnt more of that, she would have had an easier lot. But it was another one of those momentary flashes of self-consciousness he met in Sara's eyes, when she thus unexpectedly confronted him, that made him pause, uncertain how to move next in his game against her. He could not tell whether she meant defiance, or protest, or appeal. Perhaps all three. But the expression was withdrawn as nimbly as the tongue of a toad after his winged prey is secured. It was succeeded in her soft, dark orbs by a look of ingenuous welcome.

"There, you have come! I resign my task," she said, rising, while the beaming countenance of the judge became never so little blank. "Judge Irving feared you had forgotten him, and he wanted so much to be prepared for this sale on Wednesday. Don't criticize the paucity or the ignorance of my notes, please. I am only an humble understudy, who has taken the place of the leading man upon occasion."

"She has done it remarkably well, Alec," said the judge, rallying. "I may say that I never before met a lady who had her grasp of the thing. But I won't detain you, Madame Stauffer. After dinner you will give us some Chopin, perhaps."

"It is so good of you to listen. Marion and I are *so* proud of the success of our little home musicales," she said, with perfect propriety. "If Mr. Gordon is dining with you, perhaps he too will do us the honor afterward to be a listener to one of our four-handed pieces —"

"It 's not those things I care much about," said the candid judge. "It 's when you play without knowing beforehand what you are going to fall upon. By George! Gordon, that 's wonderful! If you have n't heard her, you 've a treat before you."

"If I know anything is expected of me, I invariably fall flat," said Sara, laughing, on her way out of the door.

Gordon, who closed it after her, was rather smitten with a certain meek grace of her manner,— a resignation to her position as entertaining supernumerary,— as was apparently the judge.

"Pity a fine creature like that should be put to the right about to make her own meager living," said his Honor. "Do you know, Gordon, I was meaning to consult you about an idea I 've got of asking her to — er — ah — accept compensation as a kind of — er — ah — librarian for me, and at the same time, a companion to Marion, who is never happy out of her sight."

"What do you know of Madame Stauffer?" asked Gordon, from whose path the first stone was thus felicitously rolled away.

"Know—er—ah—why—she was an instructor at Somerville College. I have often heard you vaunt the intelligence and good judgment of that faculty."

"But before? Since? I understand how Marion answers these questions; but that is not indorsement enough for the woman who is to make a permanent part of your home, and to be the guiding influence of Marion's life."

An expression that began with foolishness and ended with vexation came upon his Honor's face. His temper, always ready to explode upon being crossed or dictated to, flew to the relief of the situation. To Gordon he was simply cross, to Marion he would have been insufferably rude. In sufficiently plain terms, he announced himself quite able to take care of the interests of his household without interference from without. He eulogized the sterling excellence, above all the submissiveness of character, of the cause of their dissension; and summed her up by saying that, for a woman, she had an amount of good common sense that would keep her from making mistakes or committing follies, no matter what the provocation.

Alec, who, on the judge's outbreak of irritation, had begun to poke at a lump of cannel-coal, here succeeded in shattering it into a glowing mass, licked by tongues of livid flame that spread radiance to the farthest ends of the room. It was growing dark, and the lamps had not yet been brought in; but this enabled him to give another glance at his senior's countenance, in which he read something sufficiently startling to make him wish at once to change the subject.

A feature of the ebullitions of Judge Irving's temper was that, without opposition, they died out as quickly as they came. He was really so well satisfied with his own importance and his own judgment, it did not seem worth while to contend for them. Having sufficiently silenced Gordon upon the point under dispute, he turned the conversation to the young lawyer's chances for political advancement; upon which topic, to the exclusion of all such minor matters as women and their influence for good or ill, they talked until dinner-time.

Strémof, who had awaited Gordon's return until he could wait no more, had long ago taken his leave. One or two other people had dropped in; but Sara Stauffer did not appear. When Marion was free to go up-stairs and look for her, she found her door locked, and Sara protesting through the key-hole that she was dressing for dinner, and would join her below in due time. But Sara had not been dressing for dinner ever since she left the library. For a long time she had been pacing her floor in a stormy wrath that shook her frail figure like a reed. Then she had thrown herself across her bed and sobbed, shedding hot tears of a nature we must hope the Higher Woman will never be called upon to shed — tears of rage and defiance, mingled with overmastering love for one of the abject creatures born into the world to be woman's cross and curse! Sara may perhaps be pardoned this weakness, when we reflect that it was the first time in her thirty years of varied experience she had ever known the bitter-sweet experience of caring for another more than for herself.

When she appeared at dinner she found their party of three supplemented by Gordon, who had been induced by the judge to remain as he was, in morning clothes. Not the closest student of the human mask could have read in hers a trace of the storm that had recently swept over it. So gracious, graceful, modest, yet entertaining withal, was she, that even Gordon was drawn into the circle influenced by her. Marion, effacing herself, looked proudly on at the irresistible effect of Sara's charm upon Alec.

And the judge! What had become of the testy, elderly gentleman who usually occupied that chair at the head of the table, who either fretted at the butler about the wines, the joint, the game, the salad, or else sat in gloomy silence that fell over his household like a pall? He was gone, and in his place sat a youngish, alert, courteous, good-looking stranger, the model of a judge off duty, a judge relaxed, a genial, considerate parent, and host, and master!

So far did the little candle of Sara Stauffer throw its beams. And, after dinner, when she sat down behind the pianoforte in the half darkness of the lamp-lighted music-room, and played uninterruptedly for half an hour, Gordon felt himself impelled to go over to her side. When he reached her, he stopped short, wondering why he had done this thing.

"You won't condemn my fingering," she said audibly to the others. "I am aware that according to rule it is lamentably defective. I should be afraid to play before Baron Strémof, for example."

"But you have a gift of going straight to the heart with your music, that is of all gifts the most charming," he replied, enthusiastically.

He stood there for a moment, and, as she played louder, added in a lower tone: "I think you are a Pied Piper of Hamelin, to have lifted me from my chair, and brought me across the room, for what reason I know not."

She did not answer, but her music just then conveyed such "divine enchanting ravishment" the young man felt his steady brain invaded by something marvelously like personal attraction to the player. He wondered if it were true that, in the dusky corner where she was niched, he heard a half-breathed sigh.

The music stopped with a crash. With a petulant movement Sara arose from her seat, and passed over to sit on a stool by Marion, resting her elbow in the girl's lap.

The judge, this pretty picture in full view, was quite carried out of himself by enthusiasm.

"By Jove!" he said, gallantly, "Madame Stauffer has bewitched us all! Gordon stands there moon-struck; I believe Marion has been — crying; and I — by Jove!" he repeated, smiling ecstatically, but at a loss for further words.

Gordon, saying good night, got out into the street as quickly as possible. He had a confused idea that Marion's eyes had met his with a look of triumph, and that before he had finished shaking hands with her, she had sought Sara's face with reverent admiration. The cool air, a brisk walk down the avenue, restored his balance and made him see things as they were.

"The little Lorelei is stronger than I thought; but she has done no more than make an ass of me for a minute and a half. The question is, what *is* her game? That, I shall make it my business to find out. . . . I wonder what Aunt Effie, who is a shrewd old dear, meant by suggesting Marion will, of her own accord, come back to me. To-night she might have been a star trembling upon a lonely peak, so far away she seemed."

When he reached his room, he took out of a desk an imperial photograph of Marion which he had asked her to let him keep. As he gazed at it, a sweet, human look of love and trust he had sometimes seen there made a fresh imprint upon his heart.

"There is none like you, dear," he said loyally. "After this, either I win you back, or no woman shall claim me. And now, God speed my quest!"

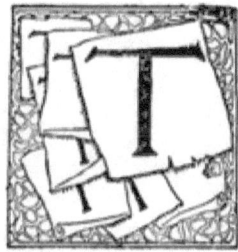HREE weeks later saw Alec Gordon again in the hall of Judge Irving's house, asking, with conventional indifference, the conventional question if " the ladies" were at home. The man who had admitted him, professing to be unaware of the movements of Madame Stauffer, said that he knew that Miss Irving had gone to attend a meeting of the University Settlement Association, as he himself had given the order to the coachman to drive there.

"Very well, Hilary," said Mr. Gordon, who was in reality well informed as to the point upon which he sought enlightenment. "Then you will probably find Madame Stauffer in the drawing-room; so give her my card, and say that I shall not detain her long."

Madame Stauffer *was* in the drawing-room. When Gordon entered that apartment, he had a sudden realizing sense of the fine way in which she had incorporated herself with her surroundings. Her face, figure, and dress had equally improved in appearance. There was in her manner a species of elegant nonchalance that allowed no hint to escape of her transitory relations with the luxury of this house and furniture.

The sun shining too brightly upon her face through a screen of azaleas in the window, she bade the servant lower the shade as though her life had been spent in controlling that servant and that shade. But Gordon, as he drew up a chair facing her, noticed that she shrank a little from his scrutiny.

"Would you not rather sit here?" she asked, indicating a place beside her.

"Thanks," he said coolly; "I took this chair, with my back to the light, the better to see your face."

"Outspoken, as usual," she answered, wincing a little, but holding her head up bravely, as she fronted him.

"Yes; I rarely lose time when I see my point, and have an opportunity to go to it direct."

"Dear me! what is it you want to say to me?" she exclaimed. "When I received your note, and made a point of meeting its request, I was plunged into agreeable curiosity."

"I have not often had a visit to make that cost me so much hesitation — so much genuine regret," he said, with a touch of honest feeling in his voice.

"More and more tragic," she replied, smiling pleasantly, "when I consider how chary you have taken pains to be of your visits, in general."

"Madame Stauffer, I am sorry for you," he went on bluntly. "But when you took up your abode in this house, you must have counted upon the risk you ran."

"Wait," said Sara, shutting her eyes. She wanted one moment alone with her own thoughts.

She knew, now, that he had found out that in her

life which she had desired above all things to conceal; and the knowledge that from him the blow of exposure was to come was more than she could bear.

"I see that you understand me," said the quiet, persistent voice.

"So it was for this you wished to see me alone," she cried bitterly. "I—blind fool—who fancied that it was, perhaps, for other things; I, who dreamed there could be such a being as a big-hearted, unselfish man that, seeing the struggle of a woman against fate, might stretch out over her the mantle of his generosity—his pity—his—but no—no! They are all alike. Cruel, implacable, they ruin and they condemn."

"I cannot imagine why you use these very inappropriate words to me," he said.

"Oh, you do not? You refuse to see what is near you,—what might have been so much to you,—what would have made of your life one long brilliant career of success over your fellow-men? How could you fancy—a man born to be a ruler—that a wife like Marion Irving, a cold, half-developed dreamer, could satisfy the needs of your nature—inspire you to great deeds?"

"It is I who am dreaming, or else you are mad that you say, or I think you say, things like this to me."

"Why should I not say them to you, as well as you say them to another, or to me? Are we not equal souls?"

"I think not," he continued, looking down upon her with a look that left her no rag of delusion as to his feeling toward her. "I beg your pardon if I seem brutal. But I cannot delay what I came here to say. I don't need to go into particulars. For some time past I have been engaged in satisfying certain doubts of mine about you, and I have succeeded. There is not in my mind a shadow of uncertainty as to the fact that you must not remain a day longer under this roof."

"Do you mean to tell *them?*" she said in a low, strained voice he hardly recognized.

"Why need I tell them? Why need I so pain her?"

"*Her—her!* it's all for her," she cried desperately. "For *her*—you have done *me* this wrong."

"If you wish me to say it, knowing your past, what in the world else *could* I have done?"

"How came you to set out in your noble quest for information about my past?"

"Because, from the first, I felt that somebody should know, better than anybody did know, who it was that had been admitted into the most sacred confidences of Marion Irving's life, to influence her thought and actions. I inquired from your late employers at the college. They referred me to some people in Chicago. The track ended there. When you were next heard of you were in the South, under your present name—*to which you have no lawful right.*"

"Well, granted that I went away with Dr. Stauffer, who had persuaded me to live according to his theories. I was deluded by a specious fanatic, a brilliant madman. I believed in him; he almost broke my heart and spirit; but he is dead. The world was all before me, the future long in which to live down six months of folly."

"People of my way of thinking have a harsher name for it," he said.

"You are pitiless! But it is over, I tell you. No one knows, unless you choose to publish it. Why is not the world wide enough for you and me?"

"It is wide enough, and I am not without pity. If you go from here at once, to-morrow afternoon, as soon as you can make arrangements to do so that will not arouse suspicion in our friends; if you will promise me to hold no future communication with Marion or her father, I shall see that you suffer no material loss."

"It needed only this!" she cried, bursting into tears.

Gordon walked up and down the room till she had spent the first force of her emotion. The experience thus coming to him of a nature divided against itself, in which an unconquerable passion for him had arisen to bear down all obstacles presented by her alleged principles of independence, was interesting enough to be dangerous to his resolution. He returned to her side, and stood there for a moment hesitating.

"You must know it is my desire to spare you anything more than it is absolutely needful for me to inflict — that makes me propose what so wounds you," he said finally. "In leaving here, you will be less than ever prepared to battle with the hardships of the world. You *must* let me help you financially — as a loan — as you will; you must not refuse me."

She had ceased sobbing, and now sprang up beside him, and laid her hand upon his arm.

"You do care, then? You care, even a little bit."

"I care? Certainly. For what do you take me?"

"Enough to give me a little longer time?" she pleaded eagerly, her face kindling.

Her eyes sought his with magnetic influence. If ever in her life, she was under the spell of a genuine feeling.

As they stood so, together, the door of the drawing-room opened, and Marion came in. Sara, who must have known who the intruder was, did not alter her position by a hair's breadth. It was Gordon who started violently away from her, and went over to take Marion by the hand.

"What is it?" said Marion, a shade paler.

Then Sara, for a moment unbalanced, sent a look of swift appeal to Gordon. But the sight of Marion had brushed all cobwebs from the man's brain. He saw the edge of the chasm he had grazed in passing. He stood erect, fearless, unmerciful — a righteous judge.

"Your friend has been telling me, Marion, that to-morrow she must leave you," he said distinctly, and without a tremor in his voice.

"To-morrow?" echoed Marion, without moving toward Sara.

"To-morrow afternoon, I think you said, Madame Stauffer? If there is anything I can do to assist you in your preparations for departure, you will command me?"

Sara Stauffer did not answer him. Turning swiftly, she swept by the two, and left them alone together.

"What does this mean?" again asked Marion.

"Marion, you trust me?" he answered, trying to take her hand, which she withdrew.

"I have had a shock," she said mechanically, going over to drop into a seat by the fire.

Gordon recognized that she would be relieved by his absence, but he could not go without one other word.

"Marion," he said, following her that he might speak in a low tone. "It's a pity you came in when you did, and it's a double pity I can't explain to you what you naturally can't understand. But I cannot. My lips are sealed. I have got to throw myself upon all the kind feeling you ever had for me. This is a pretty rough trick Fortune has played me. Surely we've known each other long enough and well enough for you to believe me, without question, when I say there has been nothing between me and that woman you might not know, if you *could* know—but you can't. She is going out of your life to-morrow, as suddenly as she came into it. Be kind to her, for she needs you. But for God's sake, believe me—and don't try to keep her in this house."

"The best kindness to me, just now, would be to leave me," the girl said; and he could see that she spoke the truth. With an inarticulate exclamation, driven from him by his thought of her vigil, soon to come, with a tremendous disillusion, he left her.

For the remainder of the day he had, about the whole matter, a defeated and miserable feeling that gave him a sleepless night. The darkness into which his wide-open eyes stared was peopled for him by visions of possibilities arising out of his interference, and the luckless turn it had taken. The scene with Sara, upon which Marion had come so inopportunely, now took on a complexion most unpleasant. What use might not that exquisitely artful person (of whose passion for him, however, it did not occur to his masculine mind to doubt the sincerity) make of the situation Marion had discovered, further to poison Marion's mind? What would it avail him to get rid of Sara, if he was to lose Marion in a way far worse than by the breaking of their late engagement? And whose part would the judge take in the matter—the judge who, having carried his point in offering to Madame Stauffer a salary as secretary for him and companion for his daughter, had found himself so evidently comfortable and at ease in the new relation?

The night, that brings counsel, did not answer any of these questions to Gordon's satisfaction. He arose jaded and out of humor; went down-town to his affairs; then into court, to be disgusted with his own performance in a particularly interesting case; and, on reaching his rooms to dress for dinner, found, cooling his little heels in the passageway outside his door, a messenger boy, bearing a note, for which he was instructed to await the answer.

The envelop, addressed in Marion's handwriting, excited so lively a commotion in Gordon's breast that he struck three matches before he could light the gas. His hand trembled as he tore the note open. But all minor sensations of any description were destined to be swept away in a flood of angry aston-

8

ishment when his mind grasped the actual meaning
of the words he read.

> Come to me if you can. I must have advice, and I have no
> one to whom to turn. My father married her to-day at twelve;
> and they have gone away on a wedding-journey. Of this I have
> just been informed by letter.

Gordon, having enlisted his good Aunt Effie to go
with him to Marion, sat that evening in the library
of Judge Irving's house, turning over and over in his
hand a letter. It was from Sara, and read:

> It is better so, my darling Marion. When I saw last night
> your confusion and distress at the announcement of my inten-
> tion to leave to-day,—when you did not come near me once
> during my packing this morning,—I was so grieved at the mis-
> understanding—I longed, a thousand times over, to tell you
> my secret, and to weep it out upon your breast. But your fa-
> ther's wishes—henceforth the law of my life—were inflexible.
> He said that in a position like ours nothing would be gained by
> previous discussion of our intention. During my talk last night
> with him in the library, when you were shut up in your room,
> he exacted from me a promise to put our plan—for which I
> may tell you he has for some time had all the preliminaries
> arranged—into execution before speaking of it to you. Ah!
> my Marion, if you are inclined to blame me, think what you—
> he—and your dear home have been to the friendless stranger,
> and say whether I could resist making them my own. When,
> after a few days' absence, we come back to you, may I not
> count upon a renewal of our sweet tie, our friendship, now to
> be one for life? May not our tastes, our aims, our energies,
> work together more closely than before? Consider, as I have,
> that in your isolated position you need me as much as I need
> you. I shall be so kind, so tender, your life will be smoothed in
> many respects, I promise. Let nothing drive from your heart
> one who, whatever comes, will ever hold you close in hers!
>
> Your SARA.

While the two women, up in Marion's room, were discussing the matter in the aspect it would present to friends and society at large, Gordon felt the sting of his defeat to be more poignant, the more he contemplated its various faces known only to himself. That Sara had effected her victory over him by a dazzling swoop, he had reluctantly to confess. For so many weeks he had carried about with him the uncomfortable knowledge of her interest in himself far beyond an ordinary interest, he had entirely ceased to apprehend danger from the direction in which it had finally and decisively come. He now cursed himself as an infatuated idiot not to have suspected that this adventuress was well equipped at every point; that, failing her schemes upon him, she would immediately resort to the act that had placed her in sacred safety forever, beyond the reach of his knowledge of her past. That, after all, was the rub. To save Marion and Marion's name from the exposure of Sara Stauffer's past, he would henceforth have to spend his best efforts in concealing it. In all human probability the question, unless he brought it up, would never present itself to threaten the peace of the Irving household. His investigation of the facts, known to few, and carefully concealed, had been made with difficulty; and even those from whom he had procured information did not suspect his object. Never did an ingenious piece of detective work reward its contriver with such a thankless ending. With all his heart he wished himself free of the secret; and then cast about him for a means of meeting a demand for explanation sure to come from Marion.

"You are still here, Alec?" said Marion, entering the room. "I fancied you would stay till I could have a talk alone with you. It was a kind thought to bring your Aunt Effie to me, and, whatever comes, I thank you for it."

"Whatever comes!" Gordon, who had risen to meet her, stood while she sat down. He had a queer feeling of complicity in the wrong that, in a few hours, had changed her to a woman of marble, with bright, glittering eyes in which there were no tears. He waited. For the life of him he could not speak.

"When you came here yesterday, am I wrong in thinking it was by appointment with — *her?*" she said.

"I had written asking her to receive me, and she had fixed that hour."

"Had you then any suspicion of her intentions to do what she has done?"

"None. It came upon me like a thunder-clap," he said frankly.

"And yet, when I came into the room, there was something between you, far out of the common," she went on, trying to weigh her words. "If it was not about my father, it must have been — on your own account," she burst out, losing her self-possession. "Oh! what is the hateful mystery? Either she is a miracle of deceit, or you—you, the one it is my first impulse to trust and believe in—have been hiding something from me. Alec, when I found myself alone to-day, in my distraction I wrote first to you. As soon as I had sent the message, I remembered the circumstance of yesterday, and I wanted to recall the note.

I think if it had not occurred to you to bring your
Aunt Effie with you, I should have asked to be excused when you came. And yet, how can I believe
you are other than I have always known you—incapable of betraying our friendship?"

"You are right, Marion. I am incapable of betraying our friendship," he said, greatly touched. "If ever
in my life I wanted to do anything, it is at this minute
to give you the fullest possible explanation of what
you ask. But it is simply impossible. For myself,
you might read every thought of my heart; but unless
you can trust me, I must go away and leave you, and
bear, as I can, the misfortune of the accident that has
placed me in this position."

"Then I will alter the form of my question," she
said, after thinking for a time. "Tell me what you
would counsel me to do. Is there known to you any
reason, apart from her duplicity to me, why I may
not accept this woman as my father's wife, live under
the same roof with her, put the best face before the
world upon the situation?"

She gazed at him steadily. The color rose into
Gordon's face. He turned aside, and walked to the
far end of the room and looked through the window
into the night.

"I am answered," said Marion, drearily.

"Marion, you are putting me in a position that
is intolerable," he exclaimed, returning to her side.
"May I not beg you, in justice to me, to withdraw
that question? Consider that you are asking me
about your father's wife."

"Then you *do* think that it is my duty to receive

her as such?" she cried, pathetically eager, it seemed to him, to cling to her last illusion. "Oh, Alec! Hard as I may seem, I am almost desperate. I want to forgive, I want to forget. I want to live down the cruel doubts I have had of her, and the constant feeling I have that she has used me, and everything around me, for her own purposes. But I can't. I will not attempt to struggle, if I must end by disastrous failure. There is only one way to meet the crisis. I must go out of this house. I cannot await them here."

"Could you not come to *me*, Marion?" he said tenderly.

"No, no, not that! Don't make me sorry I sent for you in my overpowering trouble."

Gordon started as if he had been stung.

"I did not mean to hurt you," she added quickly. "But you must see I am in no condition to talk of what I have just succeeded in putting out of my thoughts. It is not that I do not believe in you. I do; and I ask your pardon for a doubt born of extraordinary circumstances."

"I believe you never loved me," he said, cut by her measured tone.

"At any rate, I thought so once," she returned, covering her eyes wearily with her hand, as she rested her elbow on the table. "Since we have been parted, I have almost thought I was mistaken; there have seemed to be things so much more incumbent upon me than loving. In place of the heart I used to have, there is now a spot sealed under a stone. The person who has come nearest to touching it is dear Miss

Effie Gordon; but I am afraid even she will be discouraged."

"You will let Aunt Effie take charge of you?" he said, catching at a straw.

"*Your* aunt? Your nearest relative? I think not. It would only complicate matters. No, she sees that, as I do; and in the last hour she has helped me to come to a decision about my future. Feeling as I do, I cannot stay here till they return. I shall find a place to go to; and, trust me, I shall do nothing that either you or Miss Effie would disapprove of. If you choose, I will promise to be guided by her advice in everything about the change. But as, henceforth, I am to live to myself, I think I might begin now to act independently. A woman of twenty-five is no child, Alec. Don't look at me with such doubtful eyes, because I am going out to meet the world."

Insensibly, she had fallen into the old attitude of appealing to his judgment.

"What, in God's name, do you know about the world?" he burst out irrepressibly.

"It is time that I should, then," she said, with an answering spark of spirit. "I am a thousand times better equipped in means and education than most of the other women who are forced into the conflict by necessity. Is it not my plain duty to correct the defects of my environment?"

Gordon looked about the room, to whose interior of mellow beauty no sound of the street penetrated.

"And you, who have lived all your sheltered life in *this*," he said, "think you can step outside of it, alone, without definite aims, with no protection? Have you ever fancied what it would be to be left in the street at midnight, unable to get within your own door? The helplessness of woman when she is bereft of the shield of conventionality is something you never have had to contemplate, and that I cannot contemplate for you."

"What, then, do you propose for me, Alec?" she said quietly.

Gordon was silent.

"Not a residence under the roof of either of my uncles, even if their wives would have me? I can hardly go back to college — though, indeed, I have thought of teaching there, if they would make a place for me. In the seven days' wonder this affair of my father's is going to make, surely the best thing I can do is to keep out of sight and chance of comment. Miss Effie says she will help me when I have determined — and since we have been talking I *have* determined — to make a home for myself."

Gordon looked at her in surprise. In spite of the marks of deep distress upon her face, it had been lighted from within by the new flame of resolution that transfigured her.

Miss Effie, coming in, saw also the expression of Marion's countenance, and, going up to her briskly, put a kind arm around the girl's shoulders.

"Courage, my dear!" the old maid said in her hearty voice. "The hardest thing in all this world is to be true to oneself. If I don't mistake, you have been asking this boy of mine the question why you may not belong to yourself, and *perhaps* he has not been able to answer you. What you are striving for is neither unwomanly nor revolutionary; it is a thousand times better for you to work out your own experiment in your own way than to let yourself be cramped and choked by mere conventionality. And, after all, who knows but the opportunity that has come to you in this unwelcome fashion may prove a blessing in disguise?"

"You will excuse me from discussing it further," Gordon said stiffly. Just now he was irritated against all the world, including honest Aunt Effie; and his only idea of an appropriate exit from the situation was an exit from the house.

After this, he would let the women manage affairs for themselves; and when Marion should want him again, she must ask twice before he would adventure himself to a like experience. Even his dismay at the fate that had overtaken his old friend, the judge, was subordinated to the thought that Marion was now free to roam unchecked in the dangerous field of modern feminine independence.

VII

EXT morning, Marion, in her turn, awoke out of a dull and troubled sleep, to cogitate her new situation in the chill gray of early daylight, so depressing to resolutions of the night before. To Miss Effie, who had offered to remain with her, she had said no — that it was better at once to attempt the solitude henceforth her portion in life. And Miss Effie, tender, if a trifle gruff in voice, had patted her on the shoulder, told her that on the whole she was right, and, declining to have a cab or servant, had trotted off alone in the darkness, intending to catch a street-car going west.

Marion, as she dwelt on the old maid's sterling goodness, her clear common sense, her happiness in her own beliefs, yet had a little shiver of distaste at a grotesque dread thrusting itself upon her, that she, Marion, might one day come to be of the same type. Whilst combing her hair, the girl surveyed in her mirror her stately shape and clear soft coloring, and wondered if she ought to wish they would never know transformation into the square dimensions, drab tints, and tanned surfaces with which Miss Effie faced the realities of life. And yet even Miss Effie, provided by nature with a shield against contact with the wicked world, had the walls of a home behind which to intrench herself—an unimpeachable background in those faded pastels, the sisters; while Marion, having none of these, must go on her lonely way, and look not back or around her.

It would have been superhuman indeed, if, in the first moment of reaction after great excitement and stern resolve, Marion's thoughts had not dwelt upon Alec Gordon. As she lay waiting for sounds of awakening life about the house, for the soft noise of the housemaid's brushes in the hall outside her door, for the glimmering casemate to be defined upon the full light of outer day, her soul seemed to be floating afar in a world void of substance, instinctively seeking a mate with which it could blend and be at rest. This was no doubt a capital weakness, but Marion, in that hour betwixt sleep and waking, was not fully responsible. As she turned on her weary pillow, trying to banish these thoughts in sleep, again and again the image of Gordon putting aside his pride in the tender burst of pleading that she would bring all her troubles to him, with him share the odium that had been thrust upon her, returned with haunting persistence. How simple a process, how natural and right it then appeared to her, to throw aside her dream of independence, put her hand in that of this true and manly fellow, and say to him: "Where thou goest, I go. Thine is mine, the world before us is ours to meet for good or ill, to live together according to God's holy ordinance as man and wife."

God's holy ordinance! What did that mean — the
words she had so often heard over the heads of couples
standing at the altar? If there were anything in re-
ligion, was it not the first injunction of the Creator to
created man and woman, to blend their interests in
one? If there were anything in law and order of
human society, was it not the first requisite that the
joint life of man and woman should be lived as or-
dained, that their mutual love might remain immortal
in a perishable world?

Somehow or other, this was a sweet and sustaining
thought. All her other ideas of living for champion-
ship of the unaccorded rights of her own sex faded
away in the light of its steady radiance. The fond
fancies of girlhood about wifehood, hitherto dormant
in Marion, trooped up to surround the image of the
lover she had cast away.

When the maid came in, and Marion, starting, saw
upon the woman's face the ill-concealed curiosity of
her order about her young lady's changed prospects,
she was disagreeably surprised. The hard reality of
her actual lot had been, during this last hour of
reverie, so happily remote! She had had such lovely
things to think of!

Dismissing the woman, whose eagerness for items
to discuss among her fellows below-stairs disgusted
Marion, she went through the various stages of her
toilet, still strangely under the influence of the re-
bound in favor of Gordon. She recalled his trying
position under her interrogatory, his self-control, his
open statement that unless she could trust him he
must go away without her trust, and stand by the

consequences of his inability to make due explanation. Her fleeting suspicion that he had been engaged in some affair of the heart with Sara now seemed to her to have been a monstrous injustice. Whatever the understanding between them, Marion would never believe that Gordon's attitude in the matter was not one of fidelity to herself, although many evidences of Sara's fancy for the handsome young man now arose to convict Madame Stauffer of double treachery in her hasty marriage with the judge.

On Sara's side all was dark, shifty, perfidious. On Gordon's, Marion saw only his native endowment of manly virtue, strengthened by a great love for her, a love she now knew she never had deserved. The fine balance of wits and judgment in his character, his refusal ever to be moved to the right or left against their dictates, were admirable in her sight. Nothing like them was observable in her retrospect of the brilliant inconsistencies of her later friend and guide, who had ended by inflicting on her that most cruel wound.

In this mood, she went down into her morning-room to find on the table a note from Gordon, running as follows:

I cannot but hope, my dear Marion, that your afterthought of our conversation will confirm you in your generous promise to believe me without specific explanation of my share in the crushing blow that God knows I never dreamed would fall on you. If I bungled, it was hoping to be of use to you. But consideration of the affair, and, above all, of your present attitude to me, proves that I am wiser in not again offering to approach you personally. In whatever I can serve you as a friend, as a brother, as one who has received every kindness

from your father and yourself, command me always. A letter
from your father, which I found on returning home last night,
makes such explanation of his act as he thinks needful. He
asks me to convey it to you, and I do so. While I cannot, in
conscience, advise you to reconsider your intention not to
remain under their roof, I am still gravely anxious as to what
other course you will pursue. I beg of you to be guided in all
things by my aunt, who will counsel you as I could not. If I
do not again take occasion to say so, believe always in my
interest and solicitude for your welfare; count upon me not as
the lover who has failed to win you and accepts his fate,—and
to whom wisdom suggests absence from you as the only means
of enabling his judgment to act in your behalf,—but as, in the
full sense, your friend and servant,

ALEXANDER GORDON.

Marion dropped this letter in her lap.

It was as if a needle-bath had played upon her
warm feelings.

Mechanically she took up the sheet of note-paper it
had inclosed, in which the bridegroom of the day
before had penciled a few lines of palliation of his
sudden action. Few they were, and, naturally, ineffi-
cient in producing the desired result; the plea of a
vain, pompous, self-sufficient man under the spell of
a folly old as creation — determined to indulge himself, and to leave others to bear the consequence.

Her father's letter had upon Marion the salutary
effect of arousing anew her old resentment of injustice. Otherwise had she been in great peril of
shedding mere womanly tears because her lover had
at last gratified her by definitely leaving her to
herself. In a trice, the soft visions of the early
hours of day fled away from her — now, indeed, had
she attained the summit of her old ambitions; now

was she free and able to be a law unto herself! And
Marion, for the first time in all her trials, broke
down, and cried until she could cry no more.

Miss Effie, engaged with some of her charities in
the forenoon, had promised to be with her in the
afternoon.

Marion, after regaining her self-possession, was
employed in putting beneath the grate and burning
to a crisp a newspaper containing an animated
version of the surprising marriage at such a church,
by such a rector, of the well-known Mr. Justice
Irving with his daughter's "governess," when Hilary,
coming into the room fresh from a bout with a re-
porter who had called to inquire particulars of the
judge's family, brought Marion a card.

It was Mrs. Romaine's, and above the name was
penciled an urgent request to be received, if for a
few minutes only.

"That hard, cold, cynical woman!" said Marion,
inwardly. "How she will grate on me! But still—
what does it matter? I have got to face this
wretched business, and I may as well begin. Yes, I
will begin. If she is hard, I will be hard. *No one*
shall pity me!"

She went into the drawing-room to find quite
another Mrs. Romaine than the one to whom she
and society had been used. This woman's face was
not hard, and there was genuine sympathy in her
eyes, as she arose and took Marion's hand.

"My dear, as soon as I read it in my morning's
paper, I ordered the carriage, to come to you," she
said. "I felt as if I, better than some others, can

understand what has been going on, because I mis-
trusted that person from the day she was at my
house at luncheon. But, Marion, I thought it was
Gordon she aimed for,— and I still think so,— if she
could have got him. Don't think me impertinent,—
I don't mean to be,— or prying, or anything. Don't
answer me unless you like, but give me leave to talk
out what 's in my mind, or heart, rather — if I can
persuade you I have such a commodity behind my
hooks and eyes. You are dreadfully alone in the
world, you poor girl, and I came to say that if you
would like to — if you can't think of anything better
for the present — I have plenty of room in my house
for you — or, better still, if you want to go away,
I will take you anywhere — Florida, Bermuda, Spain,
Italy — all places are the same to me, and I am
always glad to move on. I have been told you
have resources, independent of your father; but don't
speak of expense. I have more money than I can
spend, and it is n't because I want a new sensation
that I ask you, though you probably will think so —"

She stopped to draw breath, and Marion saw something like tears come into her eyes, and escape upon
her cheeks.

"Mrs. Romaine —" the girl began, gratefully, her
heart kindling with a sudden pleasant warmth.

"Don't answer me yet. You 'll say no, of course;
and I hate to be refused anything. Think it over.
You won't care to stay on here — a girl of your cut
of mind and temper, I 'm sure ; and, on the whole,
the best thing would be to travel. So, pray come
away with me; and if I 'm trying, you may be trying,

too. But I'm really better than I seem. And, if you want to know one reason why I'm sorry for you — it's because I had a baby once named Marion — my only girl, whom I loved passionately. She was a wee, delicate thing, that died in my arms in her sleep. I sometimes think my husband has forgotten she was ever born; he never speaks of her. I believe he thinks it a relief to have had her taken. But *I* don't forget. I see her, in company, among the other girls; and think that if I were ever ill (which fortunately I'm not) she would sit by my bedside, and stroke my hand, and kiss my brow, and call me 'mother.' Now, my dear, I'm not given to gushing, any more than you are; but if you want me, take me, and you'll not regret it."

"If you knew how empty the world seemed to me, half an hour since, of people likely to make such an offer," said Marion, "you'd know how truly I thank you for it. When I sat there reading those wretched notices with the head-lines in the newspapers, about my father's marriage, I felt utterly alone."

"Gordon?" said the lady, eager interest perched upon her brows.

"You know, of course, that our engagement has been for some time at an end? He came last night, and so did dear Miss Effie Gordon; but I can hardly take more than sympathy in words from them."

"I thought so," said Mrs. Romaine, triumphantly. "I considered all that, before I came. Otherwise, I should perhaps not have ventured to offer myself."

"How good you are!" cried Marion, struck with this evidence of, it must be confessed, an unsuspected

9

delicacy. "But, indeed, you must not tempt me to be a coward and run away from my duties and obligations in New York. Nor must I trust myself in your home. You, who are all for the ability of woman to meet crises in life as bravely as any man would meet them, must not unnerve me at the start."

"Oh, but, my dear, a man under your circumstances would whistle and say a few bad words, and probably take a room at his club or a hotel till he had made up his mind where to move to — and that would be an end of it. He would not feel it as you do; his nerves would not be on edge at the prospect of staying here to welcome the happy couple home."

Marion shivered.

"As usual, my tongue goes too fast. No, my dear girl, what I should have advised would have been for you to make up with Alec Gordon, who, even if he does n't hit it off with me, is a rare fine fellow—"

" *You* counsel me to marry ?" interposed Marion, surprised.

This time it was Mrs. Romaine's turn to wince.

"Did nobody ever tell you that in some far prehistoric time I was in love with my husband?" she said carelessly. "Well, I was. I used to go to afternoon services in Lent and pray for that love to last, because the sensation was so much to my taste. I used to have ecstatic feelings when his foot was on the stair, and I sat sewing little baby-clothes. We lived in a plainish way then; three dollars spent in two theater-tickets was a tremendous outlay; and we walked out to dinners — I tucking up the train of my best gown under a long cloak, and laughing if the wind snatched it away from me at the corners and whipped it around my feet. Then he grew richer, and we broadened the borders of our phylactery, and then — how — when — dear knows if I can remember — we grew farther and farther away from each other. Now, when he is at home, I am aware of it because he is there behind a newspaper, but that is all! When our lips meet, it is like two pieces of dry pith coming together. I have a perfectly unsurpassed power of annoying him by my presence. I know nothing of his affairs, or he of mine. Our interests are his, not mine. Our house is mine, not his. All my tastes are 'fads'; but, so long as I don't disgrace him, he does not interfere. I have money in abundance. Money — money — who cares for money, when a man's heart and soul and brain have gone into it? How long is it since he has thought I could want anything from him but a check? But ah! if I were you, and Gordon were my suitor — if, knowing what was to come, I had it all to live over again — I think I would take the bitter present for one taste of the old sweet that can never come back."

"Nevertheless you make me feel that I was wiser than I knew," said Marion with a wan smile.

"Yes, I suppose you were wise. Now, please forget my maunderings, and think over my desire to be of use to you. If you don't wish to travel, then just come to my house, and stay with me. It is too wretchedly lonely for you here. Have you an idea when they will be at home?"

"A week hence, my father said in his note."

"A week of this? An eternity of moping. Come, my dear, I have a brand new notion. Leave the house to run itself; you have old servants who know their business. Return home with me, or come this afternoon. My husband is away; we shall be quite to ourselves. I won't let my stupid sheep-dog Loulie Kemp darken the doors while you are there, or Herr Hofman, or that idiotic Reggy Poole. Then, if you are still bent on living to yourself, we will find out a home for you, and amuse ourselves with fitting it up, and you will add an important 'one more' to the fast-growing ranks of the 'Bachelor Girls.' Oh!" and she clapped her hands, "we will make yours an ideal bachelor establishment. You shall test the question whether it is possible to do the thing properly, thoroughly, in a perfectly well-bred, unbohemian way. No divans and cigarettes like that goose Kate Collingwood, who makes such strenuous efforts to be an original, and succeeds only in being a bouncer! I am almost sorry you have three thousand a year, it would be so nice to find you a vocation. But three thousand won't go far, after what you have been used to. It will really be quite paltry, after you pay the rent of a little flat, even if I furnish it — and I have rooms full of furniture I don't use. You could not trim bonnets, could you? No, that's not your sort, at all. Perhaps you would like to be the agent to sell the violets from our country-place. The gardener tells me he has thousands in the new frames, and begs me to let him dispose of 'em."

Marion again recognized the Mrs. Romaine of her former acquaintance, alert, animated to enthusiasm in carrying out a new idea.

"There is Clara Van Shuter, who has started a mushroom 'plant' in her father's cellar, and has orders from all the clubs. She has her own floor, where she receives her own visitors independently; and is making a very tidy little income, on which she travels where she likes. Mr. Van Shuter, who is a lazy kind of a man, fond of his own ease, and not so rich as other members of his illustrious family, says he does not mind, if it keeps Clara out of mischief. Then Louise Alston runs a shop, where girls under her direction make the loveliest evening shirts for men, with white lawn ties, better than any you can get in the shops; and they drive a thriving trade. Louise takes orders at the Assemblies, and 'Howling Swells,' and the like; and supports a lot of poor women, and gives herself a nice little margin of profit. The thing is, to think of something taking; and, with a little capital, it is done. Oh, we *must* find a trade for you. I shall give a luncheon altogether for self-supporting bachelor girls, and afterward each will say a little something about her experience of the blessed estate of living to herself, and whether she can think of anything nicer."

Marion laughed outright. Mrs. Romaine had at last succeeded in putting to flight the haunting shadow of her grief.

"I can think of many things nicer," she said; "but as circumstances have driven me to making the experiment, I must try to be equal to the occasion."

"Well said, Marion! I, for one, have faith in you. And, whatever you do, you may count on me to help you."

"Then I think I shall begin by living here until my

father returns; and going out of his house quietly, to avoid the talk my leaving now would create."

"I suppose you are right," said Mrs. Romaine, a trifle disappointed. "But I shall be robbed of my visitor."

"You have a much better friend than I was before," cried Marion, warmly.

"I hope so, my dear. I need all I can get. And there is one thing certain. Your mother's provision for an independent income for you will at once determine your entity as one meriting consideration from all outsiders. If I had had any funds of my own that did not come in a stream running from my husband's pocket into mine, I should have been a happier and a better woman. If to-day I could go to work and earn an income, however small, that I might jingle in my own pocket, I should walk through life with my head higher. As it is, I spend money like water because my husband likes to have me do it; but he pays all bills, or gives me checks to pay them. I don't know what we spend, or where it comes from. I don't value it. I am a wretched do-nothing in a society of busy workers. And I 've an idea I should have made an immense success in business. Just see how I make the wheels of social enterprise go round. Ah, there was a famous wage-earner lost in John Romaine's wife!"

"I don't think I should object to owing my independence to the man I love," said Marion, wondering, as she said it, what strange influence was at work inside of her — and, blushing, she stopped short.

"Perhaps not. Unmarried girls have literally every

kind of fantastic notion before they meet the touchstone of the financial question with a husband face to face. But take my word, and be thankful for your little purse. That is the key that will unlock the chief difficulty of your present position, and a lot of others through life, I can tell you."

VIII

T was over, and Marion breathed more freely! She had nerved herself to stay and receive Sara, upon her return as the mistress of the house into which she had come in her meek poverty and insignificance, a stranger, so few months before. Needless to say, Mrs. Irving's manner upon this crucial occasion had been all that the most fastidious could have demanded. To Marion she was deprecating yet tender — not offering, but awaiting, overture; to the servants, banded together in tacit opposition, gracious, tactful, yet leaving no loophole by which any one of them might escape into open rebellion against her rule; and to her husband she held herself as to the source and fountain of all earthly beneficence and wisdom. It was long since—indeed, it had never been in Marion's experience, or in that of his present household staff— that the judge had worn such an air of complacent satisfaction with the events of every day.

Upon Marion, this new aspect of her father acted as an instant quietus of any emotional demonstration she might, in spite of her proud resolve, have been led into betraying upon his return. For the first

time she saw fully the childish side of him,— his vanity,
strutting cockerel-wise through all his actions,— and
realized that her whole life had been a sacrifice to it.
The film of filial reverence fell from her eyes. She
knew now that, had he been different, her nature had
not been warped into dissatisfaction with the common
lot of woman. Something within her even asked the
question whether, in the happy natural estate of girlhood and wifehood, where the relations with father
and husband, or other so-called "governing" power
of home, are as they should be, this modern unrest
and impatience of woman are to be found.

But this was not the time, upon the eve of putting
. into reality her most cherished dreams of freedom, to
turn and look back at what might have been. To
Sara she said nothing of her new plans. Between
those two, henceforth, there was to be a barren place,
charred as by fire, in which no shoot of verdure would
ever grow again. And Sara, who perfectly understood this fact, secretly rejoiced that matters had
turned out no worse. The circumstance that Marion
had met them, greeted them in conventional fashion,
ordered tea to be ready for the bride on her arrival,
and had sat down to dinner with them on their first
evening at home — quietly gliding out of her own
place for Sara to sit in it (which Sara did with the
most bewitching gesture of grace and deprecation) —
was an enormous gain to the new Mrs. Irving. It
had given her the *pas* with the servants, and would do
so with the outer world; and it had put the judge
into such bountiful good humor with Marion that he
was absolutely playful with her, in an elephantine way.

Sara, pleading fatigue, had contrived to leave Marion alone with her father while he was still in this happy frame of mind, enjoying what seemed to him the reward of a deed that had brought good to all concerned. And Marion, profiting by it unconsciously, for she was in the exalted state of one ready to move mountains, if called upon to do so, had gone at once to the point by telling her father that she intended directly to leave his house.

Spite of his serene selfishness, the judge was startled into an expression of some natural regret. He went further; he even lost his temper, quite in the old natural way, ill befitting a joyous bridegroom. Marion was told that she was unfeminine, ungrateful; was threatened with every variety of paternal displeasure if she so much as proposed the scheme again; and, in the end, was ordered out of his presence contemptuously, like a child who has been caught stealing jam.

"This makes it easier for me," said Marion, as with a swelling heart she locked herself into her own room. A little later, she heard outside her door a footstep, and the sweep of feminine garments. There was a soft knock, and Sara's voice pleaded with her for admission.

Marion, opening her door, stood within it holding to the knob.

"You will excuse me," she said, frigidly. "It is as well to tell you, now, that what I did in staying here to receive you was done for him. And, since he has spoken as he allowed himself to speak to me just now, there is no longer any reason to affect for you a tolerance I do not feel."

"As you like. But, indeed, peace is so much less complicated than war between us two," said Sara, with a shrug. "I could really be of the utmost service to you."

"I will owe nothing to you," said Marion, inflexibly.

"My dear child, you are always so very positive," returned her step-mother, entirely at her ease. "But I am afraid you will be forced into accepting from me your father's consent, given since I have remonstrated with him, for you to shape your life from this time according to your own desires. I don't say that I approve of it. I think that, together, you and I should have got on better than the majority of mixed families. I have always liked you, and meant well by you; and, of course, I recognize that, by living on here, and accepting me before the world, you 'd have been a tremendous help to me. But when I contrast what I was when I first came here — when you were so much more hospitable with that door of yours than you are now, by the way — with my present position and possibilities, I really can't bring myself to lament over spilt milk. Therefore, since you are bent on not forgiving me, I 'll just agree with you to carry on this thing as we 've begun it — decently, before observers. Your father bids me tell you, you are to do exactly as you choose — come, go, remove yourself and your belongings, where and when you please. This house, when you like to come here, will be open to you as before; and we shall always receive you most kindly."

"I thank you," said Marion, with haughty emphasis.

"You should really thank me, though you do not

mean it," went on Sara. "And if, as I suppose you mean to try to do, you succeed in whistling back your old lover—"

"That I will *not* hear!" cried Marion, shutting herself in her own room—to hear Sara's soft, unconcerned laugh, as she withdrew rustling down the corridor.

"What did she mean?" Marion asked herself. "It was as if she had kept that arrow for the last; and had shot it against her better judgment."

And, for the remainder of the night, the arrow, as its sender had intended it to do, rankled in the bull's-eye of the target at which it was let fly. Marion's nature, too large for petty jealousy, was just then in an abnormal and not especially healthy state of readiness to doubt every one in whom she had formerly believed. The fact that she and Gordon had so elaborately given each other up, and that she was about to embark upon the career of a "victim of arrested development" emerged into the "arena of perfect independence," did not entirely console her.

AND so, through the series of events detailed, the wrench had been made; the parting was complete between Marion Irving, her home, and her domestic duties of the past.

To Miss Effie Gordon, as the representative of Alec, she could not bring herself further to appeal for the advice and assistance offered. To Mrs. Romaine, rather, who, although she failed again to exhibit the womanly tenderness of their first interview after Marion's blow, was unceasingly kind and active in her

behalf, Marion listened exclusively, thereby wounding Miss Effie, and keeping her at a distance.

"It is only to start you, my dear," said her animated mentor, who actually put off two of Herr
Hofman's talks on Socialism, in her energy to find a
habitat suitable for her new *protégée*, "that I interfere at all in your affairs. And I have come this
morning — you won't mind that I have left no cards
for Mrs. Irving, but my time is really *so* taken up —
to say that Providence has sent us Mignon Cox,
whose silly mother has just started off upon another
one of those long wandering journeys to kill time
abroad — just the kind I proposed to you, and you
refused! Mignon, who is tired to death of dawdling
in foreign countries and being a cipher, so she says,
positively declined to go. So Mrs. Cox left her with
an ex-governess in a flat hired for her — since Mignon
could not be expected to keep up the big Cox establishment alone, and that is let at a huge sum per
annum, all of which Mrs. Cox is warranted to spend,
and more, on this expedition. I believe she and her
maid mean to go around the world, this time. Where
was I? — oh! the flat and the ex-governess! It seems
Mignon and Miss Slater have fallen out, and the
governess is about to leave. Mignon, who says she
always admired you awfully, but is rather afraid of
you, wants to know if you won't share the flat and
the expenses, have your own sitting-room, bedroom,
latch-key, and maid — only sitting at table with her.
And as she is a nice little girl (a cousin of mine,
did I tell you? — though I can't stand that mother of
hers), I thought it is just your affair."

"Mignon Cox? Why, she looks like a mere child."

"She is two-and-twenty, has a separate income from her father's estate, and yearns to be in the swim of modern thought."

"But I thought she was going to be married to Lowndes Carleton."

"So she was, but it's off. Carleton is terribly old-fashioned, you know; and when she told him she was determined not to be, according to Mrs. Browning, 'kept in long clothes long past the time for walking,' he asked her if she was going to take up the divided skirt; and that was enough. The real truth was that he scoffed at the 'woman's movement' on all occasions. Anyhow, their engagement came to a sudden crash. Of course you think she was right to rid herself of such an obstacle to progress."

"Of course," echoed Marion, but without warmth.

"This arrangement with Mignon need not last longer than the summer. It is to be an experiment, for both of you; but I know she is refined and amiable, and very affectionate; so I'd strongly advise you to consider it. Come with me now, and call on her, and you can judge how you would like the idea; and then I will take both of you home to lunch, and we can talk it over on all sides."

There was no resisting the breezy impulse of Mrs. Romaine when in pursuance of a novelty; and Marion, shortly after, found herself with that lady invading the maiden stronghold of Miss Mignon Cox.

This was a seventh floor in one of the tall new buildings of cream-colored brick — possessing florid portals of iron scrollwork, and buttoned elevator-

"PERHAPS WE OUGHT NOT TO DISTURB YOU."

men — that embody every known idea of modern architects for condensing conveniences. There were a drawing-room and a library of equal dimensions, opening out of a hall into which visitors, caught upon entering, were forced to move back or forward in single file. In one of these rooms, decorated to extremity with a colonial mantelpiece and frieze, and filled with the usual litter of choice nothings that strew the path of favored young womanhood, Miss Cox was discovered behind an Empire desk covered with brass filigree, whence she arose with cordial alacrity to receive her visitors.

That this bachelor was a pretty creature, with a complexion of cream and roses, hair purely golden unmixed with brown or red, and a physique suggesting extreme fragility, Marion already knew. They had met often in society, but in a casual way. Mignon was now attired in a so-called "morning" frock of white crépon, with floating ruffles, and a sash of white satin belted around the prettiest little waist in the world. Her hair, twisted in a small knot, was arranged with care and neatness. Her feet, shod with nicety, were matched by a pair of snowy, pink-tipped hands, soft as down, and adorned with rings of turquoise and diamonds. She had just laid down a formidable rubber penholder, of the "office" variety, which had been coursing its way unchecked over a pad of undefended paper.

"Perhaps we ought not to disturb you, dear," Mrs. Romaine said, sinking upon a "three-decker" of silken cushions, near the wood fire sparkling upon brass dragon andirons; "are you too busy to be interrupted?"

"Not at all. I was just finishing my paper upon Municipal Reform, to be read before our Twentieth Century Symposium, to-morrow. And I am glad it *is* finished, for it leaves me comparatively free. This week I had rather more than usual. In addition to my visits to the tenement-house regions, my lecture on Political Economy to a class of working-girls, whom I am really bringing over in the most gratifying manner to accept Free Trade, occurs this afternoon; and yesterday I had to lead the discussion in our literary club that takes up weekly some book of the hour."

"And what did you take up yesterday, if I may ask?" said Mrs. Romaine.

"They gave out —— —— ——, but it was voted down as really a little too advanced; then we took —— —— —— —— ——, which was unanimously accepted. I wish I knew your opinion, Miss Irving, of that deliciously sad story. Somehow or other, it seems an echo of so much I have felt and dreamed of."

"You?" said Marion, in some surprise.

"Yes, though I am not sure I should have found voice for it, had not the talented author done so for me. It makes one feel there is, after all, so little in our healthy, every-day lives of interest comparable to those of our brothers and sisters whom God has set aside for affliction and infirmity."

"When I was a girl, people used to read Molière's 'Malade Imaginaire,'" said Mrs. Romaine, with apparent irrelevancy. "And in that we were told about the learned Thomas Diafoirus, who, when he wooed his fair Angélique, drew from his pocket a medical thesis and presented it to her, at the same time inviting her, with her father's permission, to attend, as a *divertissement*, the dissection of a woman upon whom he was to lecture. That 's what modern authors are doing to you fair Angéliques, only they don't ask the fathers' permission."

"I thought you are saturated with the modern thought-waves, Cousin Adela," said Miss Cox, like a reproving cherub.

"Dear me, so I am," said the lady. "But I 'm on the down-grade in life, and I can't afford to enjoy melancholy as you can. For instance, I like to go to 'Charley's Aunt'; but you, I make no doubt, prefer Maeterlinck's 'Aveugles.'"

"That marvelous soul-drama! Oh! I have no words for it," cried Mignon.

"I thought not. Neither have I. But all the same, my dear, you are a delightful little person; and I have every confidence in your ability to make just the chum Marion Irving wants. She is n't as advanced as you, and she will be a good brake upon your wheels. You 'll give her something to interest her, and to work with. And I shall have an eye on both of you."

"I wish you would come to me," said Mignon to Marion, blushing in true girlish fashion. "I should consider it such a privilege. And I am so constantly engaged, I don't think I should interfere with you. You can have no idea how often I 've wanted to make friends with you, and how I could hardly believe my good fortune when my cousin proposed this arrangement."

10

"I am a very disappointing person," said Marion, genuinely pleased. "Could you take me soon?"

"Indeed, yes," cried Mignon. "Miss Slater is just stopping on till I can get somebody; and, to tell you the truth, Cousin Adela, she is too cross for anything. She 's one of those old bodies that always take offense at suspected affronts; and now she sits at table without opening her lips to speak to me. Oh! Marion (I may, may n't I?)—if you really will come at once, what fun we shall have!"

"Not fun. A chastened resignation to hilarious circumstance," suggested Mrs. Romaine, mischievously.

The conversation, at this point, was interrupted by the entrance of Mignon's married half-sister, a handsome young woman a year or two older than Marion, dressed with the fastidious elegance of her class.

Mrs. "Johnnie" Clyde, as she was usually called, was full of excitement, and lost no time in communicating it.

"I want you all to come to a woman's suffrage meeting at my house on Thursday," she exclaimed. "I told Johnnie at breakfast, to-day, that he need n't say a word,—that I am bound to have my turn,—and I have got several leaders of public opinion on both sides to promise to be present and address us. There 'll be no trouble about getting people to come, for the thing is a 'go' in society, if it never was before."

"And what did Johnnie say?" asked Mrs. Romaine.

"Oh! he was trying to be witty, as usual. He said

that, if, in addition to striking out the word 'male' as a qualification for voters, they require voters to be thirty-one, instead of twenty-one, years of age, it will settle the whole affair — that no woman will ever confess to the qualification."

"How ridiculously trifling men are about the great issues of our age," said Mignon, putting back into duress a truant of a curl, and elevating her little patent-leather toes upon the low fender. "But it does n't matter, in the least. Our day is coming, swiftly, surely. What if we don't master at once all the intricacies of political knowledge involved in the assertion of our rights. When we have the right to cast a ballot, we shall have wider views, see further, see all things as they are."

"Good gracious, I hope not," said Mrs. Romaine.

"Indeed we shall," chimed in Mrs. Clyde. "Mignon is quite right. It is time to have done with accepting what is handed down to us by tradition as the limit of woman's horizon. And we must work, work always. There must be no rest, no shameful peace, till we have asserted ourselves."

"Then, my dear, there will be a larger army of nervous prostrates than ever, in the field," remarked Mrs. Romaine; "for goodness knows how we American women are going to take on any more than we are doing now. That is, I confess, what is always bothering me."

"With our allotted work will come strength," said Mrs. Clyde, piously. "You must let me give you one or two 'Woman's Suffrage Leaflets' I carry about with me, Cousin Adela; and don't fail to be at my

house Thursday, at three.   You are to be one of our
champions in the column now forming for the march,
although you do amuse yourself by jesting a little
on the way.   Here is the leaflet entitled 'Wyoming
Speaks for Herself.'   It is a conclusive answer, I
think, to that exceedingly mischievous paragraph
read aloud at a recent meeting by a prominent editor
and purporting to come from an observer of the results of women's vote in that State.   And here is Mr.
Higginson's 'Short Answers to Common Objections
against Woman Suffrage.'   I wonder which of the
enemy is clever enough to dispose of *these*.   And look
how beautifully Mr. Cordaire spoke for us the other
day!   There was n't a right-minded woman present
who did n't just *love* that man when he had finished
speaking!   Why, I tell you, there are *lots* of our very
best, soundest, most conservative men ready to be
won over to our cause if we take hold of it the
right way.   As for the best women, we think we
have them already!"

"Bravo, Adelaide! I hope the husbands will all be
as amiable as yours, and then we shall have fewer obstacles.   We must get them to illustrate what they
say in that play of Oscar Wilde's that 'all men are
married women's property—in fact, that is the true
meaning of married women's property.'   As for me, I
have no more claim to that sort of property than I
have to any other.   John Romaine does n't even do
me the honor to listen, when I talk about such
things."

"But you could have us in your ball-room, dear?"
asked Mrs. Clyde, eagerly.

"Oh, yes, as often as you please. I don't think John Romaine has been inside of that room, any more than he has of our pew at church, or of my carriage, in the last twelve months."

"Never mind, Cousin Adela," said Mrs. Clyde, with conviction. "The best part of all this is that we are proving to ourselves, as well as to the men, that we can do without them."

"So we are!" cried Mrs. Romaine, looking from one to the other of the three—"except you, Adelaide, who are a high priestess. I am afraid you and Johnnie are still in love with each other."

"Of course we are," said Adelaide, bridling. "It is only that I have just come to a realizing sense of the unnecessary and unjust limitations of our sex. Miss Irving, you have kept so quiet, I wish I knew exactly your view of this matter."

"My view seems, by yours, to be a rather humdrum kind of one," replied Marion. "I think if we have the right to hold property, we are entitled to the right to vote; but it does not seem to me we are yet, as a class, well enough informed in political matters to wisely handle that right. And if all this stir should fit us for what we are seeking, then it will not be thrown away."

"Oh, I see. You are one of the moderates," said Mrs. Clyde, in a rather dissatisfied tone. "But come to our meetings, and you will get on. And now let me tell you how pleased Mr. Clyde and I are—I mean how pleased I am — that you are thinking of putting up here with Mignon. Mrs. Romaine told us yesterday she was going to beg you to do so."

"She won't be allowed to say no," said Mignon, taking Marion's hand.

"I can think of nothing pleasanter," answered Marion, looking with admiration into the beautiful eyes, appealing as a child's.

"Then it's done! You are mine! My pal, shall we say? The firm is Irving and Cox, for weal or woe — or till either of us has any valid reason to back out," exclaimed the girl, joyously.

"What is a valid reason? — marriage? —" asked Mrs. Romaine; and immediately the countenances of the new firm were overspread with gloom, tinctured with some resentment.

"There is no danger of that for either of us," said Mignon, firmly. "Now come, Marion, let me show you the flat. It's, of its kind, a perfect dear, I know you will admit. You shall have the yellow bedroom — it's larger and has the sweetest glimpse of the river over the chimney-pots and roofs; and it is n't as becoming to me as the blue. And there's a porcelain tub and tiled floor in the bath-room, and electricity everywhere. The cook and housemaid have to turn in unison when they are in the kitchen, it is so tiny. But you'll see; and I'm quite sure you'll fall in love with our bachelor establishment."

IX

MONG the political advocates of Alexander Gordon during these busy days when his prospect of high place in the service of his country occupied our hero to the exclusion of minor considerations, none was more ardent than Lowndes Carleton. Although both at the bar, the two men had never been intimate until latterly, when, during the public discussion of Gordon's aspiration to be United States Attorney, Carleton had sent to one of the newspapers a letter, since widely quoted in Gordon's favor.

This circumstance bringing them together, they had met frequently, and become friends. Gordon found in his new advocate an enthusiastic, manly fellow, as good-looking as Greek regularity of features joined to Spanish richness of coloring could make him, and, while of a pleasant temper, possessed of that pugnacity of opinion apt to be agreeable only when it chimes with one's own way of thinking.

Gordon, as he looked at Carleton one evening over the edge of a claret-glass, while they were dining together in Carleton's rooms, felt himself wondering at the heroism of Miss Mignon Cox, in having deliberately put out of her range of vision such an attractive object for daily survey; and was further possessed with a secret wish that something would lead Carleton to embark upon the subject of this his sentimental side of experience in life, which their intimacy seemed now to warrant. Needless to say that Gordon, to all intents the same man as before his final break with the lady of his own love, was still eagerly interested in all that concerned her. He knew, as everybody knew, of her removal to live with Miss Cox; and yet, by a strange fatality, he had met no one who could give him details of their arrangement, of its success or failure, of Marion's welfare, spirits, occupations. Had he, at this epoch, gone into general society, there would have been no lack of petty dribblings of information on the subject. But, partly from a natural distaste for its functions of the ordinary banal kind, partly because he preferred to keep out of range of discussions of the Irvings' household calamity, Gordon had eschewed society, and treated the houses of his friends as if they displayed yellow flags over their doors.

Moved to especial activity of speculation and annoyance by a column in an evening paper including Marion and her chum in a jocularly described list of the girl bachelors of the new era, he had arrived to break bread with Carleton in a very truculent frame of mind. Carleton, also, was perturbed. His handsome face was clouded, his speech upon all subjects was biting, uncompromising. And now, after dinner, both men had subsided into a sort of sulky silence.

"Hang it all, Gordon," said Carleton, finally emerging from a reverie during which he had been unconsciously gritting his teeth. "This is slow work for you. Let me make a clean breast of it, and say I want to murder somebody."

"Spare me till we have heard the result of the President's cogitations upon my case," said Gordon, smiling. "Then I don't know but you 'll be welcome to make a beginning with me."

"I want to know if you saw that infernal thing in the 'Evening ——,'" said his host, who declined to smile. "It has broken me all up; and you — I beg your pardon, if I take a liberty — but you must have something of the same sort of disgust and rage in you."

"Quite the same sort," said Gordon, grimly.

"If these girls were our wives — I mean if such good, straight, honest girls, who have no earthly intention to invite comment like that, would give men the right to punch heads for them, there might be a way of relieving the situation."

"As it is, we are helpless. Walter Bagehot says the Earl of Buchan once had a copy of the 'Edinburgh Review,' containing an article that offended him, put in the lobby of his house, and kicked it solemnly into the street. Perhaps you and I might insure a pleasanter evening if, between us, we disposed of the offender in that sort."

"What does it matter? The whole country will have it to-morrow, anyway. Gordon, now the ice is broken, do you mind if I talk to you about those girls? What 's the matter with 'em — with all the women, nowadays? I would not care if it was n't the nice ones — the kind a fellow wants in his home, you know; but they 're as prickly as hedgehogs, and they 're forever trumping up 'intense' arguments you are not prepared for. After I 've been in court, and down-town in that bustling throng of workers all day, I don't want to spend my evenings in a debating society where women expect you to give them the lead *because* they are women, in order to prove to you they are *not* women!"

Gordon made an attempt to answer, but his friend, having begun his tirade, was not prepared to relinquish it.

"Do you believe they are really, as they affect to be, ashamed of being loved by us in the old-fashioned way? Do you know they declare a true woman ought to teach her husband to love her ethically, not physically. Now, what do you suppose they mean by that? I don't understand; I can't understand; I am all at sea; and I confess this unrest, this hysteria they call the advent of release from their slavery of sex, is the most unpleasant feature of the not enticing age we live in."

"It is not all unrest and hysteria," said Gordon. "My own idea is that it is a serious movement that will lead to results from which many of these offensive features will be absent. But our American women have got to solve the problem whether they can accomplish all they have laid out for themselves to do. They are not, as a rule, good housekeepers; and I fear they will become worse ones. They are devoted mothers; but in a high-strung, emotional way, not always best for their children. Is the present training going to improve them in that respect? Too

many of them are but fairly good wives, inclined to
regard husbands merely as channels for golden
bounty, whose cheerful compliance and continuing
admiration of them are only their just due. I am
not sure a wider liberty will change this condition
for the better."

"See here, Gordon, as you 're in the same box with
me, I 'd like to tell you how cut up I feel about my
affair. And the worst of it is, they tell me *she* goes
about as pink and white and jaunty and smiling as
ever, perfectly absorbed in her duties to humanity at
large, evidently ignoring my existence. I could n't
have believed it of her. A perfect little angel, she
used to be. And the worst of it is, I can't go there
to see for myself how she is getting on. I said some
things when she threw me overboard that she can't
forgive, and I have n't shown myself to her since.
The fact is, I don't know whether they receive men
visitors, do you?"

Gordon, who had read in his friend's countenance
a gradual leading-up to the question put, and was
conscious of an equal desire for information of an
exactly similar kind, burst into a laugh.

"I don't know, and it 's just what I want to know,"
he said frankly, and was interrupted by the arrival of
Strémof and Clarkson, who had been asked to the
dinner, but had excused themselves on different
grounds.

"I did not join you, my dear fellow," said Clarkson,
beamingly, "because, in my new *régime*, it is really
more than human nature can endure, to sit through
a good dinner and not touch a morsel of it."

"What 's your present lay-out, Clarkson?" asked the host. "Still on that liquid food that rhymes, I believe, to hats off?"

"Matzoff? The same," said Clarkson. "And my digestion is wonderfully improved already, I assure you. The only trouble is, it is revolutionizing my habits. Hardly worth while to put on a clean shirt and a white tie and evening clothes to sit down before a bottle of milky, fizzy stuff that you have been keeping outside on your window ledge, is it? Confounded thing went off in my office the other day, and the cork hit a respectable elderly client in the eye, and scared him out of his wits. Thought it was a dynamite explosion, don't you see?"

"*You* have n't the excuse of a solitary banquet, Strémof," said Carleton, offering cigars, and a little silver lamp alight with alcohol.

"No, but I have, of all excuses, the one a man most readily accepts — the ladies," said the gallant Russian, who, having just returned from his first visit to Washington, had not seen Gordon for some time. "And in what shape my temptation came, you will never guess. I was bidden this afternoon at five to Mrs. Clyde's, to a discussion of — "

"Holy smoke! not 'women's rights'?" interrupted Clarkson, with a groan.

"Yes; and what is better, I was told to stop afterward to a 'high tea' of bachelor girls, to which the master of the house was the only other male invited. As far as I could see, the 'high tea' was a short dinner, lacking variety in wines. But the damsels — I kiss my hand to them — were lovely, most *spiritu-*

elles; they argued, they spoke, they demolished us poor men with a skill, a suavity, that made it rapture to suffer in their cause."

"What were their special topics this time?" asked Clarkson.

"The first chapter of the discourse was in insistence upon the right of women who are property-holders and taxpayers to vote upon any and all questions affecting the expenditure of moneys collected from taxes."

"Yes; but that includes all questions of every kind which concern the administration of government. And property as a qualification for the suffrage is no longer satisfactory anywhere. Even in England it will very soon come to pass that whether one shall be a voter or not will depend not at all upon ownership of property of any kind, or in any amount. If property is to vote, it is only logical that, wherever one's property is situated,— if in each of many different towns, counties, States, where taxes are applied to local expenditures,— there the taxpayer must be allowed to cast that vote; and in England, to-day, the loudest chorus of the radicals is 'one man, one vote' — to put an end to such a privilege of the owner of property."

"And next," said Strémof, "they were very animated in their demand that, if married women are to be refused the ballot, on the theory that husbands represent them at the polls, unmarried women, maidens and widows, shall not be put off on such a pretext."

"But," exclaimed Clarkson, "the law cannot dis-

criminate among women, in favor of the unmarried,
when a demand for the privilege of voting is in question; to do so would be to offer a bounty to tempt
women not to marry, or to get rid of their husbands.
There are women who would murder their husbands
to secure the right for which so many of them are
now hysterically clamoring. And there are too many
young girls already who, distracted by the agitation
for 'woman's rights,' refuse to exchange what they
call 'single blessedness' for matrimony."

"And who were there?" continued Clarkson, after
a pause, neither he nor Strémof observing that the
other men had dropped out of the conversation.

"If I could remember their names! First, Gordon,
there was your beautiful friend, the young lady who,
before any other, claimed my homage to her kind —
Miss Irving. I am grieved, but not surprised, at the
way things turned out in her paternal mansion, by
the way. And I hear that *ces dames* of high society
have not yet extended to the bride the welcome due
to her husband's place among them; but who knows
if this be so? *Enfin*, there was, with Miss Irving, a
young person of the rose and snow and gold type of
beauty one sees in our Swedish neighbors, — a ravish-
ing young person, made for smiles and laughter, but
serious as a little nun, — how she lectured us! *Ma
foi!* — what am I saying, that I ought not to say —"

"Miss Cox was once engaged to be married to me,
that 's all," blurted out Carleton. "But go on; I 've
no right to her now, any more than the rest of you."

"I beg ten thousand pardons," cried the distressed
Strémof.

"Go on with your description, and you are forgiven," said Carleton, emphatically.

"There was, of course, our hostess, a believer from whom her admiring husband can hardly keep his eyes — even when she is fulminating against his sex's tyranny. Then, two single ladies — friends who live together — who, I am told, have great wealth and a beautiful establishment, and are generous patrons of the arts. The young lady who decorates interiors; she who makes bonnets; she who grows mushrooms; the one who has kennels, and raises prize dogs for the market; one who gives lessons in whist; another who has an emporium for men's shirts; a girl of nineteen who has been coaching male students conditioned in chemistry; a firm of pretty florists; an artist or two; a *littérateuse*; a law student; a lecturer on *bric-à-brac*, in parlors — as you say."

"I beg your pardon, Baron Strémof," put in Clarkson, politely. "'Tonsorial artists' and 'chiropodists' have parlors; *we* have drawing-rooms."

"Thanks, Mr. Clarkson; but I have to unlearn in one city of America what they teach me in another," said Strémof, gaily. "Have I told you all, I wonder? I heard that each of several of these young women is in receipt of an income, earned by herself, that would support a bookkeeper, his wife, and children, in humbler circumstances; that they have great aptitude for business, great energy, and in every case behave with the greatest dignity and prudence. I wonder what old Tolstoi would say to a society like this. He would hail it with delight, *le vieux maître!*"

"That is not all 'unrest and hysteria,' eh, Carleton?" said Gordon. "Were any of these ladies prominent in the discussion of the afternoon, Strémof?"

"Several spoke briefly and gracefully. The longest speech, and it seemed to me the smoothest and best considered, came from the young lady who — er — is Miss Irving's 'chum.' She is really astonishingly suave, and looks to be hardly more than a school-girl. Miss Irving was called upon, but excused herself on the ground that she had not yet formulated her ideas sufficiently to be of weight in the discussion."

"Not yet?" said Gordon, bewildered.

When he had last seen Marion, she had been like a young archangel pluming his wings for flight into this debate.

"She avowed, very modestly and charmingly, that some of her opinions have been modified recently, and that she was not prepared to try to influence others by her own uncertainties."

"Did — ahem — Miss Cox — say anything about *her* views having modified?" asked Carleton, who had been pondering gloomily.

"Ah — not that I observed," said Strémof.

"Thank you," said Carleton, relapsing into reticence.

"I am accorded the privilege of visiting their bachelor establishment to-morrow afternoon, at tea-time," went on the Russian.

Carleton and Gordon exchanged covert glances.

"They receive, as I understand, at that hour on Thursdays, quite frankly, without a chaperon. But

Mrs. Clyde or somebody is sure to be there, *on dit;* and already their little five-o'clocks are very popular."

The rest of the evening in Carleton's rooms dragged, perceptibly. Before they broke up, Clarkson took occasion for a word apart with Gordon.

"I ought to thank you for indirectly putting me into renewed intercourse with my cousin Kit—Katherine," he said. "Since I undertook those inquiries for you, that in the light of subsequent events I could readily understand — by the way, it was lucky the faculty of Somerville had nothing but good to say of their ex-professor, was n't it? 'T would have been deucedly awkward if she had not been a fit person for the judge to marry."

"Very awkward," said Gordon.

"Has n't turned out extra well, has it? But nobody could suppose a high-spirited creature like Miss Irving would stay there and play second fiddle in that house. Noticed how sort of down in the mouth Irving J. has seemed, lately? Fellows about the courts say it 's because he has got the gray mare domesticated! But where did I begin? Ah! about my cousin Kitty. Katherine, dear soul, passed through town last week, and I danced attendance on her at her hotel; and by George, Gordon, she 's kept wonderfully fresh. I 'm an oldster, beside her. To tell you the truth, if I had n't put all such notions out of my mind, I believe I 'd propose to Kitty to lecture to *me* for the remainder of my days. But I doubt if she 'd have me; she 's just the model of a quiet, contented, young old-maid, not an ounce of

11

morbid stuff about her; and I could n't add anything to her happiness, of course."

STRÉMOF, who had engaged Gordon to walk home with him, waited no longer than until they had reached the half-deserted streets, before entering upon a subject that transformed his buoyant manner into one of sober earnest.

"I came here to-night, Gordon, to get this opportunity to consult you about a matter of great importance. I don't know whether you have surmised what feeling I took out of town with me, and have brought back stronger for absence from its source."

Gordon felt a big throb of the heart. It was the first time what seemed a possibility had been presented to him as a thing likely to happen; and it was not agreeable.

"You observed from the first what a strong hold upon my imagination Miss Irving has. She seems to be the ideal woman I have been seeking, to aid me in carrying out all the plans for my fellow-men that I have cherished from boyhood. Call me a fanatic, if you choose; it is in my blood. My father, a dear friend and disciple of Tolstoi, is full of it. I have a young sister who shares Miss Irving's progressiveness — how she would welcome her! It is n't vain of me to tell you that my position at home and my expectations would not be beneath Miss Irving's notice. I shall have large estates, wide interests, great opportunities of control of human destiny. When we first met, Miss Irving told me, with delightful frankness, of her vivid interest in my country, its problems, its people, its literature. Of me, she was good enough to say that I am more like an American than any foreigner she ever met. So I do not think that I displease her, personally; and I know that she charms me, utterly. Now, I am well aware of your former claim on her; but if that is renounced, finally, definitely, I ask you whether I have not the right to try my chance."

"You have every right," said Gordon, mechanically, though he felt a noise like rushing water in his brain.

"I thought you would say so," exclaimed Strémof, with innocent egotism. "I must tell you in all sincerity that I do not expect to woo her as an ordinary lover woos. I expect to set before her my lifework as a chief attraction. I hope to convince her of my sincerity. I can offer to her father every assurance of my fitness to ask her to be my wife; but, I forget — it is no longer a question of offering to the father — I shall have to ask *her* to weigh me in the balance, and see if I be found wanting. It is in fact a comrade — a fellow-missionary — that I am seeking to take home with me; but that will not prevent my loving her, and being to her what one of her own countrymen would be. Smile at me if you like, Gordon, *mon ami* — I shall not resent it. I have, no doubt, a way of expressing myself fervently, that you self-contained Americans do not understand. But I am sincere, *voilà tout.*"

"I believe you, Strémof," said his companion, upon whom it was now clearly incumbent to make appropriate answer. "And it's no use my telling you I understand your feelings. That would be highly superfluous."

"But you see that I could not go on further, without this sanction from you ?" cried Strémof, whose radiant zeal made him eager for the relief of speech. "You, who, of all the men I have met in this wonderful, inspiring country, are the one I should first choose to be my friend always."

"You are very good," responded Gordon, secretly possessed of a desire to end their friendship then and there by some such indefensible act as knocking Strémof down.

But this was not because he did not, in spite of bitter rivalry, appreciate and admire the honest spirit of his unconscious opponent. He was overpowered by the new idea that danger, like this now threatened, could have come to him from such a quarter. Such a thing as Marion's loving, or giving her hand to, any man of their common acquaintance in New York had never suggested itself. He knew her too well; there was no other possible Richmond in the field! She was cold, fastidious, a dreamer of dreams, isolated by her fancies from risk of impressionability from ordinary sources. It was only some great quixotic enterprise, some task to work out, some definite career to accomplish, that could tempt her. And here was this winning and ardent thoroughbred, appearing to offer just what, under the circumstances, might prove to be, to her, a welcome outlet for her energies.

"I do not ask you, my dear Gordon, to give me your good wishes," pursued the young man. "It is too much; because, whatever the cause of your separation from the lady, I well know you cannot be pleased to think of another man winning that prize."

"Confound his impudence!" was Gordon's thought, as he assented with some unintelligible monosyllable that might have meant anything.

It was perhaps well for both of them that the conversation came to an end in their arrival at the door of Gordon's lodgings. He did not ask Strémof to go in, nor did the latter seem to expect it.

"*Vous ne m'en voulez pas*, Gordon?" he said, as they parted, with a boyish appeal that upon another subject would have won a cordial response. "You won't keep a grudge for me? You think I have been, as you say, 'fair and square'?"

"Altogether fair and square," said Gordon, giving him his hand.

Strémof, humming *Carmen's* song, heard at his first meeting with Marion, fared gaily off into the night. Gordon, on his door-stone, watched the blithe fellow disappear, and then mounted his stairs, feeling as if a leaden weight were attached to each foot. Opening his desk, he took out, as he had done on a former occasion, Marion's photograph, and again gazed at it, but with a different feeling.

"You did not reclaim this from me!" he said to her, in spirit. "You knew you could trust it with me. And, to prove that you were right, I now surrender it."

A fire was burning behind a wire-gauze screen upon his hearth. Removing the screen, he realized for the first time the chill of his fingers and of his heart.

Bending down, he threw the photograph upon the

coals.   Strangely enough, it fell erect, and shriveled from below, leaving her lovely eyes gazing at him untouched.

He could not resist an impulse to pluck away the fragment, and, scorching his fingers in the act, thrust the remainder of the card into destruction.

"Finis!" he said, aloud, the smart of his burn recalling him from dreamland to the infirmities of poor physical nature.

After this, he knew, it would be no more in him to make a step in her direction until she should ask it, than for the obelisk in the park to wander forth to pay court to Diana on the tall tower.

X

PRIL had come, and winter, lingering in the lap of spring, found in the household of Judge Irving hardly a realization of expectations so fondly cherished by the newly married pair upon entering into their bond. Over the master of the house, indeed, had passed a change that was patent and consoling to his domestic staff. In the tart language of old Ann, an Irish-American citizen who had been long a resident under his roof, "He was that bruk in sperit, praise the saints! 't was a joy to see him about the house." The new mistress, who had been regarded at first with considerable doubt, had succeeded in planting her banner triumphantly upon the kitchen citadel. The servants, one and all, swore by her, enjoyed her liberal reign, her love of luxury, and the stir and vivacity her presence had brought into the previously dull house.

For although Mrs. Romaine and other ladies of Marion's acquaintance had somehow not yet found it entirely convenient to pay their respects to the judge's bride, there had not been lacking a following to the representative of his name and fame. It is

curious how, in a large society, such a following is
formed. It is gathered from unexpected quarters; it
presents to casual view a very fair imitation of a select original whose doings are constantly upon its lips;
and yet, turn it as one may, the hall-mark is nowhere
to be found. And Mrs. Irving had not by any means
intended to frequent a society that had not the hall-
mark. What she aimed for was to leave behind forever the debatable land, and to come out into a region
of unshadowed respectability. She even hated some
of the people she had drawn into her circle, so dubi-
ous did she feel them to be. But, all told, she did
not hate them as much as she did the people of
Mrs. Romaine's set, who resented the unseemly haste
of her marriage with Marion's father, and, although
they could extract no word in blame of her from
Marion, were persuaded that Sara had ventured
among them out of her place.

Everything is forgotten or lived down in six
months in New York, Sara had heard it said, and
with that she was obliged to be content. In the
mean time she was not going to live exclusively
dependent for companionship upon a vain, pragmati-
cal man, whose demand upon her for approval and
compliment was practically without limit. Why, this
would be worse than the boarding-house in Washington, with the old ladies knitting and speculating
over the society columns of newspapers! Luckily the
hours were long in which her lord kept himself and
his sponge-like appetite for praise down-town; and
there was Marion's carriage for her to drive in, and
Marion's vogue in the big shops, that she had once so

much envied, to draw upon. But even this, and the obsequiousness of shopmen who did not know the difference between herself and the "real thing," became in due time a bore. Her eager intellectual spirit cast aside the acquirements of material wealth as heartily as it had aspired to them. The safe haven of conventionalism now hers — for she had little fear that her Nemesis would ever rise up to hound her out of it — seemed to her already at times a prison.

To do Sara justice, the governing impulse of her discontent was repudiated love. As well as she could love any two beings, she had loved Gordon and Marion — Gordon, fiercely, imperiously, with a first passion unsupported by reasonable hope; Marion, fiercely, jealously, and, withal, with a certain reverence for her regnant quality of womanly purity of thought and word and deed. Sara could not tell whether she would rather have had Gordon return her feeling, and thus alienate her from Marion — or have Marion believe in her and trust her as of old. Now that she had lost that trust, it seemed as if an angel, stooping toward her, had been suddenly snatched away.

In her first resentment of Marion's very natural inclination to shrink away from her father's wife, Sara had tried bravado, had assumed indifference. But in reality she was stabbed to the quick with disappointment. How could she let Marion know that the marriage with the judge had been like a plank to save her from drowning? Upon the episode with Marion's lover, Sara chose not to let her memory dwell.

The fact that Gordon also had kept aloof from
her since her return as his old friend's wife did not
of course surprise her.   His visit of ceremony — two
cards left one afternoon when she was sure to be out
— had not been followed up, and she had lent her
subtle powers to the work of estranging her husband
from him.   When one considers how easily this process is every day accomplished, in the matter of husbands' friends, by women who have no such good and
cogent reasons as had Mrs. Irving, her success is not
surprising.

Sometimes, as the days went on, and Marion did
not come back to her, Sara sat fretting her heart out
in a desire to reclaim the girl's love and respect.
From what she could gather here and there, her step-
daughter, under the new influence upon her life, had
blossomed out to be quite a different being from the
recluse of her father's home.   Marion was heard of
as in demand by society, not of the madly merry
variety, but of such cultured and individual folk as
Sara would have given her eyes to call her own.   And
now there had come to Sara's ears a surprising rumor
concerning Marion — a rumor she properly judged to
require investigation before it was believed.

The story had been brought to her by a certain
Miss Boulter, a girl like herself on the fringe of a society she yearned to enter, but, unlike Sara Irving, a
silly, pushing creature who carried her small wares
of gossip like a packman from house to house, and
was at no time, in the handling of them, redeemed
by the saving grace of wit.

"Is it possible you have n't heard?" said Miss

Boulter, with well-simulated surprise. " I thought, as much together as you and Miss Irving are, you — I just admire Marion Irving! She and Mignon Cox were at the play in Mrs. Romaine's box last night, and Baron Strémof was there, too. He 's a beauty, don't you think? Something so aristocratic — I wish you 'd have him at one of those nice little dinners of yours, and ask me. I think he 's ever so much better-looking than that ill-mannered Alec Gordon, who undertook to pretend he did n't see me when I bowed in the street the other day. But then blond mustaches are so much prettier than dark ones, don't you think so? Popper says I 'm so gone on foreigners he believes I will end by marrying one myself, and, if I do, he 'll not give me a cent. He says they are all make-believe titles and fortune-hunters, every one of 'em. Does Baron Strémof expect to get a lot of money with Marion, I wonder?"

"Baron Strémof is a man of rank, culture, and wealth," said Sara, stiffly. "He is, besides, of a charming temper and manners, and an offer from him would be an honor to any girl to whom he should make it. But you will oblige me by not asking me to discuss the affairs of my husband's daughter with an outsider."

"Goodness me!" Miss Boulter observed, retiring under cover of a spiteful laugh. "I could not suppose it was such a sacred matter, seeing you had n't even heard of it before I told you."

Sara, mentally determining to cross Miss Boulter off her poor little visiting-list, came to a quick resolve. Ordering her carriage, she drove at once to

the cream-colored mansion that held her stepdaugh-
ter enshrined on its seventh floor, and, boldly ascend-
ing in the lift, pressed the electric button of the
Bachelor Girls' door. A plump little maid, with a
butterfly of white muslin soaring above her head in
lieu of cap, ushered the caller into Miss Irving's sitting-room, and, taking her card, announced her intention to "see" if Miss Irving was at home.

Marion came at once, a look of alarm upon her face.

"My father — there is nothing the matter with
him ?" she asked eagerly, holding back perceptibly
from Sara's studied smile of greeting.

"So you think nothing short of illness or accident
would have brought me ?" Sara said with a gentle
melancholy in her tone. "I come, my dear, as an
envoy from your father. We have heard that your
engagement to Baron Strémof is discussed as likely
to be, if not already, a fact, and we think common
propriety demands that we should know how much
of this is true."

"When my father makes such an advance to me as
his child deserves," Marion said haughtily, "I shall
answer him, not you."

Even Sara's armor was not proof against the look
that accompanied this speech.

In one of the revulsions of mood that lent, in its
way, an odd attraction to her character, she went
over to Marion's side, and took her hand tenderly.

"O Marion, why can't we be friends? If you knew
how weary the days are that keep you from me; if
you knew how all I have acquired seems as nothing
beside the knowledge that you shun and mistrust me!

"MARION CAME AT ONCE."

After all, what have I done that another in my situation would not have done? Why should you sit forever in the seat of judgment, and condemn a homeless pauper who accepted such bounty as your father offered me? Put yourself in my place — everything in the world I aspired to do was dependent on means and opportunity — could I refuse them? Marion, Marion, forgive me, and love me as you loved before."

"It is not that I cannot forgive," said Marion, slowly. "I believe, if I know my heart, I have already forgiven you. As affairs stand, it has all turned out for the best. My life is freed of some of its worst crosses. If I am not altogether happy, it is because no one in this world is meant to be happy, I suppose — " she stopped, sighing.

"Take me back into your heart, darling, make me your confidante as before, and I'll engage to make you 'altogether happy,'" cried Sara with her old impulsiveness, throwing her arms around Marion, and kissing her upon the cheek.

But Marion, troubled and unresponding, drew away from her with a movement of repulsion Sara could not mistake — a movement that, while it pierced her with mortification, aroused in her an impulse to repay it in mischief.

"So you will have none of me, eh?" she said in a changed tone. "Well, as you please. But, before we drop the subject, tell me, to clear up mystery, if the grudge you bear me has nothing to do with the little interlude between me and a certain old lover whose place you seem so quickly to have supplied."

Marion started violently. Sara could not now complain of her indifferent exterior.

"You don't answer, but I do not need words. Pray, then, when *you* had no longer a claim upon Gordon, why should you have resented what you supposed to have passed between *us?* Had not I, as well as you, a right to my chance? To tell you the truth, he was so much a man that, had I not realized the match with your dear father had been made for me by heaven, I might perhaps, by now, have been in enjoyment of privileges you cast away."

"Is this true?" said Marion, coming nearer to her.

"What can it possibly matter to you, now?" returned Mrs. Irving, gracefully.

There was a pause. Marion was trying to control the emotion that confused her power of formulating thought into words. Sara was rapidly reviewing contingencies.

"For not only," went on the stepmother, "did you give him up, in the first place, for no reason that anybody could see, but you have chosen entirely to break with him since."

"I did not choose; it was his doing," said Marion, forlornly.

"Indeed?" said Sara, quickly, having thus ascertained exactly what she desired to know. "But, my dear, when you know men as I do, you will understand that, however kindly Gordon may still feel toward you as a friend, it would be natural for him to keep his distance till all these things have become a little more ancient history. Men are not fond of being confronted with their own changes of base."

"He told me," said Marion, impetuously, "that there had never been anything between you and himself that I might not know—only he could not speak. And I believed him. I believe him still."

"Hum! Admirable! Just what I should have expected of him. He belongs really to the age of the *preux chevalier.* *If* you believe him still, my dear girl, then why should you have asked me if what I hinted at were true?"

"You took me by surprise. But now that you have gone so far, you must say all. Tell me what had happened between you the day I came in—the day before your sudden marriage with my father. Had Alec—was it a question whether you should not rather marry *him*—oh, why do I ask that? Don't answer me! I promised to believe him. It is your manner that is trying me beyond endurance. You seem so full of something I must have been blind to —well, then, *do* answer me!"

"I cannot deny that some such question was discussed between us," said Sara, dropping her eyes, "though it is hardly becoming in your father's wife to speak of it to your father's daughter. But I insist, Marion, that you put to me no more of these explosive questions that grate upon my nerves in the most hateful way. Let us talk, rather, of your intended marriage, which you have left me to assume is no idle rumor. As the Baroness Strémof you will have a brilliant position and a husband of an ideally sweet temper. You two will have abundant opportunity to go tilting together at windmills. On the whole, your life will have a great deal more local color in it than it would have had as plain Mrs. Alec Gordon, the wife of a New York lawyer. I almost envy you the opportunity of getting out of this little frog-pond we call New York society."

Then Marion rallied.

"What, already?" she said; and the famous "Déjà" of Talleyrand did not sting deeper. Sara had actually nothing more to say.

Marion escorted her to the door of the lift, and bade her a courteous "good morning." As the lift sank out of sight with the little richly clad figure, wearing an air of almost dejection, Marion had an impulse to call after her some word betokening regret. But the image of Gordon came between them, and the softened moment passed. She went back into her room and wrote a note; then, ringing for a messenger, despatched it firmly.

Mignon, returning later to the house, found her chum sitting before a wood fire that was twittering like a chimney full of birds. How long Marion had been there, she herself did not know. As Mignon spoke, she started in a bewildered sort of way.

"Surely you have n't been asleep?" said Mignon, laughing.

"I—I think not. Why, how absurd—of course not! I have been reviewing my whole life, dear—all my opportunities, my aspirations, my disappointments. And I have been wondering whether I can do better with what remains of it than to take up a definite mission to help poor souls in chains, and at the same time make somebody happy who is fonder of me than I deserve."

"Marion, listen to me," said Mignon, throwing off her jacket and hat, and dropping on a chair at Marion's side. "You don't love Baron Strémof; you are trying to work a mine that has nothing in its veins. Regard, respect, romance, are not going to make up to you for the love you do not feel."

"Why, Mignon!" said Marion, regarding her with astonishment.

"I know you think I 'm a selfish and heartless little cat; and so I was. But this winter, spent for other people, has set my mind to working on many things that did n't occur to me before I was out of leading-strings. I used to take my mother's views as gospel; now I see I have a right to my own. I believe every woman's life is given to her for her very own. I don't mind telling you, now, that if mama had not disliked Lowndes Carleton and kept disparaging him to me at every opportunity, I should not have parted with him. Mama's own married life was wretchedly unhappy, and I suppose I reap the fruit of it. But it was n't myself I started to talk about. I wonder if you would let me ask you one little question. Are *you* ever sorry you gave your lover up?"

"'*You?*' Oh, Mignon!" said Marion, putting one finger upon her mentor's roseate cheek.

"Never mind. Tell me, Marion."

"It would be no use telling you, if I were. It is he who gave me up, really. Something is between us that is too dark and sad for anything."

"And you are no longer interested in Gordon?"

"Did I say that?"

12

"Enough, perhaps, to be glad he has got his appointment. I met Mr. Clarkson in the street just now, who told me a telegram has just come from Washington saying that the Senate has confirmed the President's nomination, and that Gordon's friends are all jubilant."

"I am glad," said Marion.

"Really, Marion, I don't know what to make of you. Yesterday you would not have spoken of it in that lifeless way. But no more of Mr. Gordon.

"I will tell you of my visit this morning to my little German woman,—the baker's wife, you know,—with the week-old baby. I was sorry to find that since I was last there she was not doing so well. The woman who was taking care of her had left, and Mrs. Stromeyer was very restless and miserable, the baby crying, and the place dreadfully upset and dirty. It was that, as much as anything, that worried her, I saw; and so I went to work and had a regular 'clean house' on my own account, aided by a stupid girl I impounded on a lower landing of the tenement and paid, then and there, to help me. I always liked bringing order out of chaos. And when the rooms were clean, and the husband's breakfast things washed up, we set to work upon the invalid, who besought me to give her baby a good bath. I don't think I ever touched such a young creature before, and I was rather timid; but the mother directed me, and there were clean clothes in a drawer. By and by I had the little thing as fresh and pink as an arbutus bud; and dressed it; and, to stop its wailing, laid its cheek against mine as I walked up and down the floor. Marion, did you ever know how soft and sweet a baby's cheek is, and its little fuzzy head? I wanted to hug the darling tighter, but it would not stay quiet with me, and so I laid the little bundle beside the mother, and instantly the crying stopped — such a funny little gobbling noise, and the mother radiant over it in spite of maladies, dire poverty, husband out of work, she quite unfit to nurse her child! I stopped at our hospital, coming back, and made arrangements to get her in there till she is well again. Marion, that baby really felt and smelled like a rose-leaf! I shall never marry, of course; but I had a sort of a little thrilling feeling of what motherhood must be. It is so strange, you can't imagine — no one can imagine — till a baby is left all alone in one's arms to care for. I could have stayed there for hours, for the pleasure of feeling its warm body upon my heart. I wonder if Mrs. Stromeyer does n't have that to balance some things you and I have, Marion. Oh, dear! there are all those circulars to address and get out this afternoon. And here comes Mary with a note for you. No answer, Mary? Then you may go and serve luncheon at once. Now, Marion, as I live and breathe and am a curious girl, that 's Strémof's crest upon the envelop!"

"It is an answer to one I sent him a little while ago," said Marion, coloring deeply as she opened the note. "I think I will leave this with you, Mignon, while I go to prepare for luncheon. But don't comment on it to me afterward, please, dear."

Left alone, Mignon's eager orbs lost no time in

possessing themselves of the contents of Baron Strémof's epistle.

"Your word is law to me," it said, "and I leave
town this afternoon, for a fortnight in Boston, without attempting to see you. But unless you notify
me, there, not to return at all, I shall count the
hours before placing myself again and forever at
your feet."

Miss Cox made no attempt to overcome the blank-
ness of her feeling. After thinking it over, she rang
the bell, and interrogated the butterfly-topped maid.

"No one has called this morning, Mary?"

"Oh, no, miss; only the circulars that was left by
the Ladies' Suffering man; and the Cruelty Society
called for the bundle o' clothes; and Mrs. Irving for
Miss Irving, miss."

"*Mrs.* Irving?"

"Yes, miss; a pleasant-spoken lady, in a rich brown
velvet suit and hat. I don't think she's ever called
here before now; but I made sure 't was a relation,
and let her right in; and Miss Irving saw her right
away."

"Yes, Mary. Luncheon, now."

XI

HILE Strémof, in Boston, was enjoying a wide variety of discreet hospitalities that went as far as possible toward robbing this especial absence from New York of its sting, Gordon, in the excitement of his honorably won success, felt a sense of something lacking to his satisfaction.

But a short time before, the household to which it would have occurred to him to carry his laurels, for the best kind of congratulation thereupon, would have been the Irvings'. Now that door was closed to him. The judge had, indeed, indited to him a short perfunctory note, expressing his satisfaction at the final action of the Senate in Gordon's case. But it was not a note that referred hopefully to any meeting of the sender and recipient in the immediate future, and Alec could not but feel it confirmed the previous distance between them. Harder to bear was the absolute silence of Marion. Unreasonably ignoring that it was he who had elected total separation from her as the better part of discretion for him, he worried himself with daily expecting from her a few words of kindness that never came. So many little missives *had* come to him from fair women with whom he could claim only the passing acquaintance of society. On all other sides the world exposed to him a broadly beaming smile. But from Marion, nothing; absolutely not the ghost of a conventional word of approval.

With an idea, perhaps, of obtaining some tidings of her, he repaired one Sunday afternoon to call upon Mrs. Romaine. As he drew near the familiar front door he even indulged in a hope that he might meet Marion within, and his brain grew dizzy with the fancy. Hear from her, or from somebody, he must, of the progress of Strémof's suit. Strémof absent in Boston, Strémof silent, uncommunicative, did not seem much like a triumphant lover; and yet the uncertainty was intolerable. Gordon had even worked himself up to the point of being afraid to take up a newspaper, lest he should somewhere come upon an announcement of their engagement.

Mrs. Romaine's surroundings, that afternoon, were unsatisfying. There was about the rooms a scattering of the mixed lot of her acquaintances. The hostess, in a robe of gray satin with big muslin sleeves like a bishop's, sat against a mass of orange cushions, and poured tea. But she seemed distracted, looked wan, talked to make talk, was a trifle more brilliantly vague than usual. On a gilt chair at her side Reggy Poole, her familiar, sat babbling with infinite importance about nothing in particular. He was a well-dressed, fat-faced young man, with a little mustache above a baby mouth; and black hair parted in the middle, and glued to his head like a priest's cap. In season and out of season, even if nobody listened, Reggy must always talk. He would hold on to his hostess's hand on arriving at a ball, and keep back the stream of people behind him, while he told her a little anecdote of himself last year at Homburg.

On the other side of Mrs. Romaine, who was doing the honors to a foreign ambassador imperfectly acquainted with the English tongue, were two ladies profoundly interested in each other's oracles; that is to say, they were talking for the most part together. By close listening, only, was one able to ascertain that they were exchanging experiences about a new prophetess of faith-cure.

One of these disciples, a long, slim woman with flaxen hair, pale eyes, and a little shining knob upon her long, slim nose, gesticulated a good deal with a pair of long, slim, pearl-colored kid gloves; but her face showed no change of expression. When for a moment she would pause, her companion, a chubby little lady, "greatly infested with beads" in her costume, would dash in eagerly to tell how she had been raised by faith from the bed of unprecedented languor to which she had been abandoned by all the faculty of physic.

Another group enshrined a fashionable woman of letters, who looked like a Polish princess making her first round of the American republic; two or three of her adorers; an artist of American birth and Parisian residence who had returned to enjoy the fruits of his renown in a brief glimpse of home; and Mrs. Townsend Murray, an agreeable widow oscillating between two hemispheres, of whom it was claimed that she dined at her own house only when her chef was ordered to provide for a company of invited guests.

Elsewhere people were less interesting. Herr Hofman stood alone beside the mantelpiece, on which he had set his cup of tea, dipping into it sweet biscuit, which he afterward absorbed with solemn gusto. There was no trace anywhere of the object of Gordon's search.

Gordon, stopping by the tea-table, shared the privilege of his hostess's conversation with the foreign ambassador for a while; then, declining to be buttonholed by Reggy Poole, he strolled on to the party to whom Mrs. Townsend Murray was now dispensing animated speech.

"I have signed nothing; I shall join nothing," she was saying with finality. "The only compensation a woman can claim from society for getting on to be fifty years old is the right to be amused by it; and I don't find this women's suffrage business even amusing. But then I have lived down so many 'movements' in New York. I have been shaken to my center by such a variety of enthusiasms. Long ago there was a society of 'The Crescent and the Cross,' in which what was called the liberality of American thought gave precedence to the Moslem symbol in the title. I believe it was to furnish relief to the hospitals in the war of Russia against Turkey. At any rate, it nearly disrupted our body social, and there was a dark whisper that all or much of the fund raised was pocketed by remote agents of distribution. Then we had an early dress-reform wave that was dashed and lost on a question of becomingness.

I never even heard what became of that; but we quarreled frightfully while we were getting it up. Then the 'Centennial' agitation, and one can't have forgotten the tantrums *that* raised; and a half-dozen others I won't bore you by recalling. There must always be something that women of our class, unconvinced of on one day, will rush into with an absolute rage of conviction the next. And we generally begin proselyting before we acquire the articles of our faith. Vote? No, thank you; I decline. I might be willing to deposit my own vote, but I don't want it to go in and be lost under those of my naturalized French, German, Swedish, Italian, and Irish maid-servants. And I don't want them going to the clergy for instructions how to vote."

"Right you are, Mrs. Murray," observed a feeble voice. It was that of young Mowbray Packer, chiefly known as the rapid dispenser of his father's hard-earned millions, and for paying an enormous price to secure an artificially tinted gardenia, fresh every day, for his buttonhole. He was small, pale, bald, and had a heart discoverable only because of its occasional rebellion against the incessant smoking of cigarettes. "Can't think what the women mean by undertaking to put themselves on a level with us, you know! Wish people would stop agitatin' things, anyhow. It 's no use. World 's all played out, seems to me."

"That 's lucky for you; don't you think so ?" said Mrs. Murray. "Mr. Gordon, you are a man of the future; is it your opinion the world has gone to the dogs ? "

"I am too busy in my own part of it to look far

away from me, I 'm afraid," said Gordon. "But I think the standard of mankind and womankind keeps up pretty fairly."

"Don't you think the women are a little ahead of the men?" put in a sharp young woman who was under Mrs. Murray's wing. "Has not your race degenerated? One used to hear of men doing gallant deeds, and looking like heroes, but there are n't many such around my way. There are only athletes, now, who perform in public—for universities; and they soon go out and belong to the dead level of men who seem to do nothing but try to make or spend money."

"Allow me to refer you to our late war," said Gordon. "That afforded examples of heroism that ought to be remembered *at least* half a century. But perhaps you will be better able to appreciate something more nearly contemporaneous. Am I allowed one little story of to-day, Mrs. Murray? I promise not to be long. Last year, in the Matabele war in Africa, a small party of Britons went into the bush to intercept and capture bad King Lo Bengula. Only recently the story has been published which explains why none of that little company ever came back. A Matabele warrior has told how they met their fate. The Englishmen, surrounded by overpowering numbers, fought till their last cartridge was exhausted —some shooting themselves rather than fall by the hands of the savages. A little handful of the wounded survivors, who had been partly sheltered behind dead horses, then dragged themselves, bleeding, together, and stood shoulder to shoulder in a group facing the foe. 'Then they raised their hats,' the

Induna is reported to have said, 'and sang that song of your country I have heard the missionaries sing. And, as they were singing, our warriors swept down on them like a river, hurling their assagais as they ran, and overwhelmed them, and speared them to death.'"

"And what song did they sing?" asked one of the women.

"It was 'God Save the Queen!' And perhaps you remember a similar incident, when our own flag-ship, the *Trenton*, was wrecked at Samoa a few years since. The crew, assembled on the quarter-deck, expecting death, sang the 'Star-Spangled Banner' while the old war-ship was driving on the rocks — to destruction, as they believed; though, happily, they were saved to sing another day."

"Quite so!" remarked Mr. Mowbray Packer, strolling away from the group to seek entertainment elsewhere.

"It does seem as if the men have a little showing, still," commented Mrs. Murray upon Gordon's recital, "and as if Odin had n't kept all the heroes of the sagas to himself. I fancy most of the charges that men are degenerate in our day come from women who for the first time find themselves thwarted by their lords and masters in little schemes of their own. Now, I 'm a free lance. I have n't any lord and master, so I am lifted above suspicion of truckling in such a matter. I own I like men rather better than women, at most times. And why do the women suffragists say men have deliberately retarded their efforts? That does not seem to me fair play."

"What men have really done, in this generation and locality," said Gordon, "has been to concede to women everything they have themselves been agreed upon as reasonable or desirable to demand as a right. The indifference of women generally to the claim of a right to vote is what chiefly retards the efforts of the champions of the female suffragists; and the open and avowed opposition of others is the obstacle they cannot overcome. When women all move together in that matter,—or in any other,—Heaven defend those of my poor sex who attempt to stem the current!"

Mrs. Murray and Gordon had been left to themselves.

"I must take this opportunity to tell you, Mr. Gordon," the lady said, "how proud *this* representative of our party is of your having won the prize. You know I am a bit of a politician, unfashionable as that is with us. I have watched you, and know of your progress in affairs. Perhaps, in the sweet by and by, I shall be one of your lieutenants in a campaign to make you President of these United States. Only I am afraid there will then be, as they threaten, a woman Vice-President upon your ticket; and I have long ago sworn never to work again for women."

"Perhaps you yourself will serve on the national ticket with me," said he, smiling.

"Dear me, no; there might, by that time, be the disability of age, among others, for me. I can think of no one woman among the ranks of the suffragists who would do to put forward with you, unless it were that stunning-looking Marion Irving, whom I hardly

know—the girl who is living with Mignon Cox—
daughter of the judge who married his—type-writer,
was n't she? Now that Miss Irving might be made
anything symbolical, monumental; but I did hear—
it seems to me the ambassador told me a few moments ago—that Baron Strémof is to marry her."

"Is this generally known?" asked Gordon, not a
muscle of his face betraying that he had got the
death-blow, dealt so heedlessly.

"Bless me, I can't tell you! One hears so many
things. Old Roncesvalles loves gossip, and must
always have a crumb of it to distribute as he goes.
Ask him. No; he 's gone. Ask Mrs. Romaine.
She 's by way of being intimate with that pair of
pretty spinsters. You know Strémof, then? What
a dear he is! So refreshingly unaffected in this age
of manner; and so full of appreciation of the best
there is in us! Why—almost everybody 's gone!
I did not know it is so late. Did you happen to
see our host come to that middle door just now, and
stand for a moment by himself, looking at the people
around his wife, then disappear? He looked absolutely ghastly. I am afraid the poor man is ill, so
we had better take ourselves away. Tell my girl
over there I am going, please."

When Gordon went up to say good-by, Mrs. Romaine asked him in an undertone to remain until
after the others had gone. Struck with an expression of her eyes, as if she were keeping at bay some
mortal apprehension, he noted in amazement the absolute self-control with which she fulfilled the last
fraction of her duty as a hostess. Then, as the ser-

vant let fall the portière held aside for the departing visitors, she motioned Gordon to a seat beside her.

"You are not well ? You are in some anxiety that I may relieve ?" he said.

"Am I ? Perhaps. I did not know that I show it. I kept you to ask if you have heard this story about Marion and Strémof, and if you are going to let the thing go on."

"What can I do ?" he replied icily.

"It is a sort of pious insanity on her part, I think. Oh, Mr. Gordon, I have n't the grip on things I once had, or I should stand up and proclaim to young women, nowadays, the gospel of letting true love light the flame on conjugal altars. I begin to think if we called back our talents from the turmoil of out-door affairs, and devoted them to what the Lord gives us for better or worse, at home, we 'd be happier. And why should Marion even contemplate this marriage, when I believe her heart and soul are yours ? Go to her; it is never too late to right wrong. Break up this affair."

"How can I ?" he asked, flushing, but with his lips still sternly set.

"Oh, I don't know. Everything 's an insoluble problem in these days. There 's that pretty little cousin of mine, Mignon — made to be the joy of some fond husband's life; she 's another devotee to the ideal. But I, who have tried everything, and failed in everything, who am I, to preach to them ? They would laugh at me if I told them that in every natural woman's life the need of loving and being loved by man is the immortal impulse, sure to overmaster

her some day. Now, I 've prattled enough; you
think I 'm an impertinent old woman. Go away,
and let me rest for a moment before I dress for
dinner."

"There is nothing in which I can personally serve
you?" he said, holding her hand and looking her in
the eyes.

"No, no."

"If the moment arises, you will promise to think
of me?"

"How good you are! I ought to have had a big,
strong son like you."

"Is your—is Mr. Romaine's health quite what it
should be?"

"I think so. He seems quite the same, only
bothered by affairs. Are n't all men bothered by
affairs? As a matter of fact, probably, you know
more of his concerns than I do. If you ever marry,
Mr. Gordon, open your heart to your wife, and let
her stand beside you, not apart from you, in interest.
Now, good-by again."

Gordon, pondering on these things, repaired, after
his dinner, to his Aunt Effie for a chat. The kind
lady, too wholesome to nurse a grudge, did not call
him to account for recent neglect of her. She talked,
instead, and with hearty interest, about himself;
soothed his ruffled spirit; and finally led him to tell
her outspokenly of the wound corroding in his
heart.

"I heard it to-day," said Miss Effie, looking blank.
"And, my dear, if I were of the crying sort, I 'd
have cried—then and there. She 's your girl, Alec,

cut out for you in heaven, and I don't understand this sudden, fantastic alliance with a foreigner."

" Strémof is *sui generis*," said Gordon, hastening to do justice to his friend.

"All the same, I don't believe in it. I know very well it 's because I 'm your nearest relative that Marion has kept away from me. I don't resent that— though I 'm sorry. If I could, I 'd stretch out a hand to help you, Alec, boy."

" Help me ? What do you mean, Aunt Effie ? Do you suppose I am a child, to fret after another's prize ? Thank God ! I 'm no weakling ; and, if I know myself, this is the last time I shall speak to any living being of her personal relation to me. Please to consider that chapter ended, and the covers clasped."

Miss Effie had something on the tip of her tongue, but, like the heroic woman that she was, kept it there.

Alec, picking up a new book from her table, fell to discussing that.

After he had gone, Miss Effie opened a compartment of her desk, and, taking out a faded ambrotype of a soldier in uniform, looked at it for a long time.

XII

N the camp of the Amazons, now threatened with a disbandment so unwelcome to Mignon, had arisen a spirit of determination on the part of that small campaigner which boded ill for the gallant Strémof's hopes to secure an American bride.

Whatever the world might assert upon this subject as final, Mignon knew the matter was not yet closed. She was aware that three days yet remained of the fortnight's probation, at the end of which Strémof might be allowed to claim what he aspired to. She had given up talking about it with Marion, but, by watching narrowly, saw that her friend was every day more nervous. How heartily Mignon wanted to cut the knot of difficulty by the simple process of bringing Gordon and Marion together, only she knew. For days it had absorbed her thoughts almost to the exclusion of her platform and her work of canvassing for emancipated women. Had she lived in the artless days of old, she might have followed the method then pursued by ladies desirous of securing the presence of an unwilling gentleman—hiring bravos to abduct him after dark.

13 205

But, short of this compelling device, she saw none
that would accomplish her desire. The little obstacles of conventionality are surely to blame for the
gravest miscarryings of human affairs. Knowing
for how long a time Gordon had absented himself
from Marion, would Mignon be justified in inform-
ing him that Marion was—unconsciously perhaps—
as much in love with him as she was repentant of
her pledge to Strémof?

Mignon tried to persuade her chum to write to the
absent suitor, and tell him frankly she had made a
great mistake. But Marion was in an exalted state
of devotion to supposed duty. Strémof had convinced her that life with him would open a broader
opportunity for usefulness than any she was likely
to find at home. The prospect of living out of
New York, and at the same time doing missionary
work among those " most interestingly wretched "
Russians upon Strémof's estates, kindled in her an
excitement she almost mistook for pleasure.

A wise mother, to whom Marion might have carried her case in this exigency, could have demolished
its weak points with love and common sense. But
what was Marion's only counselor—poor little Mignon, her own head stuffed with distracting aspirations and mistaken aims, with noble fallacies, with
puzzling counter-impulses—to advise? Had they
not, together, many a time decided that duty to the
individual should be subordinated to duty to society
at large? Whatever their personal discomfort, must
they not, before all things, assist in running the
machine of the Brotherhood of Humanity?

But as the days narrowed into hours before Strémof was due to return, Mignon grew unaffectedly desperate to keep him away. In the throes of conflicting feelings she walked over to the hospital to see after her Mrs. Stromeyer, the wife of the baker out of work, and joint proprietor of the bewitching baby.

Things there were in a bad way for the house of Stromeyer. Not only did poverty still hold the husband hard and fast in its clutches, but the wife was sinking fast. While the baby in another ward slept, all unconscious of his distressed estate in life, the husband, admitted behind the screen around the cot, sat dazed and wretched at the patient's side. The doctors who had just passed on their rounds had told him she would not last out the hour.

Mignon, laying aside the useless cluster of spring blossoms she had brought, stood sorrowful, looking on at this little scene from the drama of every day. Presently the sufferer, opening her eyes, became aware of her visitor, and smiled gratefully.

"That is nice! I am happy," she whispered, her eyes quickly leaving Mignon to seek her husband, her wan hand going out to imprison his.

"Sh'an't I bring the baby?" asked Mignon, seeing the end was near.

Obtaining leave from the head nurse, she ran away into a far ward, and, returning with the infant in her arms, leaned down to let it touch the mother's lips.

"That is nice! I am happy," repeated the woman. But she did not look a second time toward the child. Her gaze again sought her husband.

And as Mignon left them, the man's head had fallen forward upon the bedclothes, the wife's arm was around his neck.

MIGNON went out of the hospital into the broad sunshine of the jocund day, and walked home slowly. In the seclusion of her room she wrote a note, and sent it by special messenger.   Just what influence the pitiful scene at the hospital had in shaping this course of hers she did not allow herself to think.

For the remainder of the afternoon she was restless, growing white and red by turns, starting at every ring of the door-bell.   Nothing she ordinarily found interesting attracted her.   She even renounced an important lecture, to stay indoors, seeing Marion go off to it with ill-disguised satisfaction.

"If any one calls, I am at home, Mary, you will remember — at home," she enjoined upon the butterfly maid.   And — shall it be told of her? — Mignon then selected from her wardrobe a gown, not of the most recent cut, but undoubtedly enticing to the eye — a gown long hung away under others, and twisted anew her golden locks to place the knot at an angle formerly much admired by interested eyes.

This done, she was wrought up to a pitch of excitement that brought on internal tremblings, ill masked by apparent calm.   She tried to read; tried the piano; she rearranged the flowers, the ornaments on the mantel-shelf; then — last resource of expectant woman — changed the position of several pieces of heavy furniture.   At length, bethinking her of an unfinished essay for a girls' club that was lying upon her desk, she boldly took up her rubber penholder, and dashed into a sentence left incomplete:

"Not, O my sisters, until woman shall cease crying out against her wrongs at the hand of man, and set herself to living as if man were not, shall—"

Here the clock struck five, and Mignon jumped. Dropping her pen, she turned around to interrogate the clock-face, as if trying to persuade herself it was in the wrong. But it was a very well regulated little timepiece, and obstinately held its own. Five o'clock —and she had said she would be at home to him at four!

To Mignon's dismay, two round, bright tears welled in her eyes, to course their way adown the rose-bloom of her cheek. It was a crisis at which any girl might have been excused for an expression of temper against things inanimate. The first object Mignon's eyes rested upon was her uncompleted essay; and, tearing the page from the pad, regardless of wasted wisdom, she crumpled it viciously in her hand, and threw it into the fire.

Simultaneously there was a ring at the door-bell of the flat—an insistent, energetic ring, short, sharp, and decisive. Mignon's little heart fell to beating so violently she could hardly breathe. She felt herself wondering if such an internal tumult could possibly show *outside*. But she retained sufficient self-control to give a glance into the little mirror above the mantelpiece. The door opened. It was the maid, preceding a gentleman.

"Mr. Carleton," said Mary, secretly pleased that this visitor could not, by any stretch of imagination, be converted into one of those "Ladies' Suffering" men of whom she was beginning to be aweary.

Lowndes Carleton did not smile overmuch when Mignon held out her hand to him. He was, at this period of his career, in the condition of the dog Dr. John Brown tells about, of whom his master averred:

"Oh, sir, life is full of sariousness to him. He can never get enough o' fechtin'."

"I received your note about half an hour ago," he said with business-like gravity; "and as it seemed to indicate some matter of importance, I came as fast as I could get up-town."

"You are very kind. But I knew you would be," faltered Mignon, as they sat down on opposite sides of the room. This distance, however, was not so great that Carleton, by extending his long legs, could not easily have succeeded in covering half its width. He studied the crown of his hat, while she, the ready speaker, the silver-tongued oracle of women's meetings, wondered, now that she had him, what use she could make of her acquisition.

"It is a hard thing to explain to you why I have asked you to take this trouble," she said at last. "I don't know whether it will make it any better if I say it is for another person — other persons — friends of yours and mine, who I think are in great distress that might be remedied if I only knew how to do it."

"I could hardly flatter myself you would send for me on your own account," said he — with unnecessary irrelevancy, Mignon thought.

"It has been so long since we met, I did n't quite know whether you would recall my name," she answered — also going off the track with an unpardonable deviation from facts. " But that is neither here nor there. And, not to take any more of your time than I need, let me tell you at once what I mean."

Carleton now lifted his eyes from the crown of his hat, and looked at her. Then Mignon's eyes drooped; she took a paper-knife from the table, and began playing with it upon her lap.

"We—my friend, Miss Irving, and I—have heard how much your partizanship did for Mr. Gordon in his campaign. I felt sure you admire and appreciate him as all his friends seem to do. And I wanted to ask if you— if you think —would it be possible — if you know whether— he is in town," she broke down lamely.

" He is in town. I saw him to-day at luncheon. He is very well, very busy, overrun with necessary affairs, and one of the best fellows in the world," Carleton's lips said. His thoughts were concerned with their tumultuous recognition of his favorite gown, his favorite mode of hair-dressing. But he did not know quite enough to take these, upon this occasion, as a tribute to himself.

"I ought to tell you, I think," Mignon went on, warming to her subject, "that, after I wrote to you, I was frightened to death lest I had done what Marion's delicacy would take offense at. You know— maybe you don't know— she is one of the most fastidious girls I ever met. But the only thing, in such a case, is to apply it to one's self— and I—"

Mignon stopped, appalled. She ventured a glance at Carleton, to see what effect her slip had had upon him; but his face gave her no satisfaction.

"Won't you go on with your statement?" he said, returning to his hat, she to the paper-knife.

"It would be better to ask you what you would think of a pair of people — who, I believe, truly love each other — getting apart for no really good reasons (though they seemed so at the time), and then not being able to come together again."

"Well?" he said eagerly, his eyes kindling with sudden hope.

"Suppose the girl had never been truly happy since their parting, and it was *not known* that the man had — er — formed any other attachment — "

"Of course he had n't," Carleton blurted out.

"You really think so?" cried Mignon, ecstatically.

"Think? I know it. By Jove! where would he have found a girl that could hold a candle to her, even if she did play the mischief with his feelings?"

"But she did not mean to, and she has been wretched ever since — perfectly wretched almost all the time."

"Mignon!" he exclaimed, making an abrupt movement by which his stick, entangled with the fire-irons, knocked them over with a crash.

"Why, Lowndes, how awkward you always are!" she said quite naturally, stooping to put the poker and tongs in place. "Yes, wretched; though she would n't have had anybody know it for the world. And now that a crisis has come in her affairs — "

"A crisis?" he said, turning pale.

"Yes; she has given a conditional promise to another man to marry him. And to-morrow the other man is coming: and if nothing interferes, she will be bound forever. And, oh! how I can look on and see my poor dear mistaken Marion — "

"Marion?" he thundered.

"Lowndes, don't be so noisy! The servants will hear you in the kitchen. You would never do in a flat."

"But you frightened the very life out of me with your hypothetical heroine, don't you see?"

"I don't know what you mean," she answered, overcome by the old familiar methods into which they had involuntarily fallen. The sound of his voice seemed to her as joyous and inspiring as a bugle. To be near him stirred in her an old delight in living she had quite forgotten.

"You are acting in a very odd way," she said reprovingly; "and, unless you sit down again quietly in your chair, I can't finish what I began to say."

"You need n't finish; I understand," he interrupted breathlessly. "You are for showing me there's a chance for Alec Gordon to get his sweetheart back; and, to satisfy you, I 'll promise now that I won't leave a stone unturned till I bring him here, dead or alive, this evening. Losing her just took the salt out of his life. And, whatever has happened between them since, if he thinks she will have him again, he will come fast enough."

"I don't know that she would like him to think exactly that," cried Mignon, rather alarmed. "A girl could n't well ask a man to come and just talk things over, could she, no matter whether any good is to come out of it? But no, no! I have no authority to say that Marion wants to see him."

13*

"You think it likely?"

"Ye-es," she said finally, laying hold, as upon an anchor, of the paper-knife.

"You believe there is a moment in a true, honest girl's life when she is ready to put aside nonsense and affectation, and own to the man she has wounded that she is ready to make him forget it all in an eternity of bliss."

"Oh, Marion would never forgive me saying *that!*" she exclaimed, her face dyed with innocent blushes.

"Let Marion go, Mignon. Let Gordon go. For this little minute think of yourself and me, and tell me if all you 've been saying for *her* does n't apply to *you* too, dear."

"But *I* 'd never have sent for *you*," she cried, on the verge of tears. "Never, never; and you know it! If my mother were here, it would be different."

The sight of the poor little Bachelor Maid breaking down in a fit of crying in her chair appealed to the best manhood in her lover, and took him, at two strides, across the room away from her.

"I shall go now, dear," he said, with his hand upon the knob. "Don't fear I will presume on your generosity to her. But it 's given me hope; and after I 've succeeded—as I shall, I promise you—in doing what you want, perhaps you 'll not forbid me to come back on my own account."

Mignon wiped her eyes, and took courage.

From that moment dated her conviction, since unshaken, that whatever life-work a woman has to do, she does it better for sharing it with man.

MRS. ROMAINE came in to dine with the girls that evening, saying her husband had sent word from his office he might be detained away till late. Neither she nor Marion could account for the extraordinary rise in the barometer of Mignon's spirits. The little maiden was transformed into a creature full of tricksy merriment, her joy bubbling, in spite of her, into all she said and did. Marion, whose wings were tipped with lead, could not follow her friend's flights. In her heart she thought Mignon for the first time a little flippant. Mrs. Romaine, also, was grave and preoccupied. It was a dull banquet, between them; and as they sat afterward around the fire in the drawing-room, even Mignon's gaiety flagged. From time to time she glanced at the clock, and sighed.

"What ails you, dear?" said Marion, finally. "One would think you bewitched."

"You and I are brakes upon her wheels," said Mrs. Romaine, rousing herself from painful abstraction. "Come, Marion, give me something pleasant to think of. Tell Mignon and me if to-morrow is really to see you promised to be the future Baroness Strémof."

"I have asked for another day," replied Marion, blushing deeply.

"Thank Heaven!" cried Mignon, clapping her hands.

Mrs. Romaine could not resist a shaft of her old forging.

"Reprieve at the final moment! The prisoner mercifully spared for further consideration of her offense? My dear girl, you know your own affairs, but, for Heaven's sake! let a thousand Strémofs be disappointed rather than do yourself the wrong of going into this with any uncertainty."

"But I am certain," said Marion, proudly.

"Then, in that case, I retire."

"I am certain of so many things that make others seem less important," the girl went on more gently. "Dear Mrs. Romaine, have confidence in me. I have not found life so full of sunshine that I am likely to rebel if I sometimes wander into shadow in the future."

"What a way for a girl to talk, in anticipation of her married life!" Mrs. Romaine thought; but she did not speak this thought. Instead, she looked at Mignon, and was surprised to see that young lady's recent exaltation of spirit succeeded by a look almost woebegone.

"What's in us all?" said Mrs. Romaine, shrugging. "Depend on it, girls, this is what it will be like when we have finally downed our tyrant man, and undertake to get on without him."

There was a ring, and Mignon's color came back into her pretty face. Her eyes shone, her cheeks dimpled.

"Let us agree, then, if these are some of the said tyrants come to call, to make them welcome — no matter who they may be," she exclaimed saucily.

"Judge Irving, for Miss Irving," was the altogether astonishing announcement brought to them.

Marion's face was pale, her lips firm, as she walked across the entry into her own sitting-room.

She found her father wandering about the tiny place in his top-coat, having forgotten to remove his hat. He looked shrunken, careworn — denuded of dignity, of importance. Marion, smitten by these facts with compunction, offered to kiss him; but the judge seemed hardly aware of that overture of friendship.

"She has gone away from me, Marion," he said, without preamble. "I don't know for how long. I shall never be sure she does n't mean to come back. She has long shown me she was tired of my life — tired of me. Yes; she 's been restless a good while. But I was not prepared for her leaving me."

"I am — sorry," Marion began to say, and paused.

"That is not the worst. I believe she is going on a lecturing tour in Canada and the Northwest! She showed me a letter from an agent — and a poster, Marion, calling her 'Mrs. Judge Irving of New York'! It is rough on me, though I 've got nobody to thank but myself. She 's been making it very hard to live with her, my dear. There are two women in that one; you 've never seen the worse. And it will be hardly possible to tell when she may not be coming back."

He sank into a chair, so dejected and crestfallen that Marion could scarcely believe her eyes.

"I am sorry, father," she said again presently, going over to lay her hand upon his shoulder. "Don't think I blame you for what has kept us apart. We both made mistakes. It seems to me life is all mistakes."

"There 's another thing I came to say to you, my dear. From something she let fly, in a fit of anger with me, I think she flatters herself she has helped

to keep Alec away from you. If she said anything
against him to you, Marion, I'd — I'd take it with a
grain of salt. She has not scrupled at falsehoods.
And I could see there was some angry feeling in her
boast of this to me.

"You believe he was never in love with her?" she
cried eagerly.

"Never, my dear. On the contrary, he did everything in the world to warn me against her, for your
sake. All he did was always for your sake, Marion.
I did hope you and Alec might forgive bygones, and
be friends with me again — and with each other. He's
a safe fellow to trust both you and the books to after
I'm gone; and there'll be a good lot of money. But
she said you are going to marry the Russian. Is this
true, Marion?"

"I believe so, father," she said, in a low tone, her
hands straining one within the other.

A tap on the door. Mignon was there, a radiant
look upon her face.

"I would n't disturb you, dear; but here is some
one 'who wants to see you, and your father too, on
very particular business. Please go in, Mr. Gordon;
Mrs. Romaine and I will take care of Mr. Carleton!"

A few moments later, the judge went away from
his daughter's door, and walked dejectedly down a
long avenue, to bring up at his club. He slept there
that night, and, after he was in bed, tried to remember just what had passed before he had left his
daughter standing hand in hand with Alec Gordon.
He had an idea that Gordon, on entering the room,

had taken Marion at once into his arms, and that Marion had seemed more than content to let him do so. But to his Honor all minor events were swallowed up in the flood of mortified vanity and crushed pride that had overwhelmed him.

MRS. ROMAINE, yawning over a magazine in the dining-room, remained at her post as chaperon of four happy people as long as she could keep awake. Then, breaking up the ball, she ordered the men away, asking Gordon to accompany her in her brougham as far as her own door.

It was only a short distance to her house, and Gordon had hardly begun to tell her of his capture by Lowndes Carleton, who had pursued him half over town in a cab before finally coming upon him at dinner with a friend, when the brougham stopped.

A servant, evidently in waiting at the front door, ran down the steps to meet them. He begged Mrs. Romaine to go at once up-stairs to her husband, who had entered the house but à short time before themselves, looking so ill the man had wanted at once to send for a doctor. This forbidden peremptorily, Mr. Romaine had shut himself in his own room, whither nobody had yet dared to follow him.

"Let me wait and keep the carriage in case you should need a doctor," suggested Gordon, startled not so much by the news as by the look of apprehension upon Mrs. Romaine's face.

"Thank you, perhaps it will be best," she said; and he saw that her thoughts had flown before her up the stairs.

"Does she care for him so much?" the young man wondered, entering the library, and sitting down to ponder on his own surprising fortune. With Marion's kiss upon his lips, Marion's plea for pardon in his ears, the affairs of other people could not seem to him of the first importance then.

Before long he had a message from Mrs. Romaine, praying him to go up to her husband's room.

"Mr. Romaine is better, I hope?" he said to the butler, who preceded him.

"Can't say, I 'm sure, sir. I did not see Mr. Romaine himself," the man answered imperturbably.

What was it? Gordon felt a sense of uncomfortable anticipation as he followed along the corridor, and tapped at the door indicated to him.

It was opened by Mrs. Romaine, who, drawing him inside, shut and locked it. Gordon looked at her in dismay. In the brief time since their parting a terrible change had been wrought upon her face.

"My dear lady!" he exclaimed in a shocked voice.

"He is there—in his own room—you will see him presently," she said in a lifeless voice. "Sit here a moment, first. I must tell you what soon every one will know. My husband is not only a ruined man—he tells me he is disgraced. He says he has ruined so many others that, after this, men will always speak of him as a thief!"

"Good God!" cried Gordon.

"There is more. When I got up-stairs, a few minutes ago, I was just in time. Another minute—there would have been—*this*." She faltered, and with a shaking hand lifted a pistol from the folds of her dress.

Possessing himself of the weapon, Gordon made haste to unload it, and to place the wretched woman in a chair, where, dropping her head upon a table, she gave way to a burst of sobs and tears.

"But I must tell you all," she said, when again able to articulate. "No, how can I tell you, when I myself don't know particulars? For weeks I have seen that some awful cloud was over him; but God knows I never dreamed of this. Of all the chances of misfortune, this would have been the last for me to expect. I always believed in his integrity among men — always — always. But he has told me now, everything — freely, fully. Oh, would to God I had shown him long ago what he is to me, and he might have confided in me when there was yet time to save him and his victims! He did n't mean wrong, Mr. Gordon; I 'd swear to it. See how generous he has always been to me, to every one! It was that mad rage for speculation. It has overwhelmed him and all who trusted him. And now that, like a child, he has opened his heart to me — what shall I do to comfort him, my love, my poor darling!"

Another storm of despair swept over her. Gordon, standing beside her, kept his hand upon her shoulder tenderly, firmly.

"When he thought of dragging me down in the disgrace that will be known everywhere to-morrow, his impulse was to get out of life — anyway, he said. He supposed, oh, God! that I would be *relieved* — relieved of my husband, the lover of my youth — my

poor husband, weighed down with sin and care!
Think of that, Mr. Gordon! Think I let him believe
so! It breaks the poor remnant of my heart. But
I 've saved him from the worst — I saved him. He
is mine still, to comfort, to stand by — no matter
what 's to come!"

There was silence, broken only by a fresh burst of
her uncontrollable love and sorrow. Gordon spoke
at last.

"You are quite sure he will make no other attempt
to —" He glanced significantly at the pistol still in
his hand.

"No, no. He has promised to live for me. He is
in there, lying across his bed, not stirring. He has
given me leave to speak to you."

"My dear lady, this is inexpressibly painful to me,"
began the young man. "Perhaps you will tell me
what you would have me do?"

"Do?" she cried, springing to her feet, with a look
of dauntless resolve in her haggard eyes. "There
is but one thing to do — thank God we are childless!
As I have told my poor darling, we must face it —
and meet the punishment — together!"

WHEN Gordon, late that night, found his way from
the rooms in which he had undergone a most dis-
tressing experience, he passed unobserved through
the lower hall deserted by the servants, who scented
disaster.

As he let himself out of the stately portal, and
stood for a moment in the vestibule, he lifted his hat
toward the door.

"To the Higher Woman," he murmured, then strode with a sad heart from the house around which shadows deeper than those of night had forever closed, into the brightness of his own steadfast way.

In the contemporaneous aspect of their affairs it is possible to give only a few facts in disposing of the other people with whom this episode has had to deal.

Just yet it is hard to say what effect Strémof's disappointment has had upon him. He met it with, assuredly, an admirable bearing, sailing shortly afterward, with the remark that he will return to pursue his studies of American sociology.

The junior member of our firm of Bachelor Maids very soon became an utterly devoted Mrs. Carleton. As they were giving up the flat on May 1, and her mother was remotely heard from as still upon her travels, with no intention of abandoning her pursuit of change of scene, Mignon decided that she could do no better with herself than be married from the house of her sister, Mrs. Clyde. Lowndes, as soon as he had secured his individual share of female suffrage, stopped fulminating against it, and was spoken of by his wife's friends as "an ardent sympathizer, only not quite ready to speak out." The worst recorded against him was a query to his wife whether, on the whole, she considered that she would have done better by defeating nature than in letting nature defeat her. But, as Mrs. Clyde observed, it is hardly worth while remembering the foolish things men say when they are trying to make you think they feel themselves your equals.

Marion, while awaiting her own marriage, fixed for the early days of June, had returned to her father's house. She there told Alec and Miss Effie that, in thinking over her winter's experience, she had come to regard the woman question as one involving the whole—not half—of the human race.

"So do I," said Miss Effie. "I regard our emancipation as an inevitable development awaiting us, but one in which men are equally concerned."

"You are willing to let us think that, in helping you out, we are working for our own regeneration?" asked Gordon. "Well, be it so. I recall those lines of Tennyson:

> The woman's cause is man's: they rise or sink
> Together, dwarf'd or godlike, bond or free:
> For she that out of Lethe scales with man
> The shining steps of Nature, shares with man—

Here my memory fails me. What comes next, Aunt Effie?"

"I can remember only this," she answered, looking at the two with eyes brimful of satisfied pride:

> Till at the last she set herself to man,
> Like perfect music unto noble words."